FILIPPO, ME AND THE CHERRY TREE

Paola Peretti

Translated by Denise Muir

HOT
KEY
BOOKS

First published in Great Britain in 2022 by
HOT KEY BOOKS
4th Floor, Victoria House
Bloomsbury Square, London WC1B 4DA

Owned by Bonnier Books
Sveavägen 56, Stockholm, Sweden

www.hotkeybooks.com

Text copyright © Paola Peretti, 2022

This is a work of fiction. Names, places, events and incidents
are either the products of the author's imagination or used
fictitiously. Any resemblance to actual persons, living or
dead, is purely coincidental.

A CIP catalogue record for this book is available from the
British Library.

ISBN: 978-1-4714-1105-2

also available as an ebook

1

Printed

Hot Key

FILIPPO, ME, AND THE CHERRY TREE

ALSO BY PAOLA PERETTI

The Distance Between Me and the Cherry Tree

Dreams

Dear Estella,

It's been nearly three years since you went away to my beloved cherry tree, the one outside school, to live with Grandma Alba and Cosimo.

I know, now, that all the stories I used to tell myself (and still do, given that I'm sitting right here in front of my computer, writing to you using my voice) are just that – stories – made-up things to make me feel better.

I'm getting a bit more used to the dark now but I still get scared sometimes, so it helps me to think about you, how we got to know each other, all the things you'd say to comfort me, to help me see things more clearly.

I know, now, that you and Grandma aren't real any more. Cosimo, the boy in Papa's favourite book, The Baron in the Trees – *he was never real. At least I don't think so.*

Today I'm having one of those difficult days I mentioned. I've no idea why, but it feels like I'm going to have that weird dream again about the tribe of girls. I need your help, Estella.

Do you remember the first time we met? Olga, the eye doctor, had just told me my eyes were going to switch off eventually (great news, eh?!), so I'd climbed up the cherry tree and even broke my glasses.

You were cleaning the school at the time, and you found me. Not long before that, I'd found Ottimo Turcaret, my cat (he was just a kitten back then) up a tree in Grandma's garden. This time it was you, someone from far, far away, who was there to get me down from the tree. You had come all the way from Romania to find a best friend! A girl who was practically blind and scared of everything, even of climbing down from a cherry tree. How about that!

Now that I'm properly in the dark, I love going back over in my head all the times we spent together, you telling me stories about Amazons and vampires while we snacked secretly on packets of crisps. It helps me, and makes me sad at the same time. Is that even possible? You'd say of course it is. You'd say that nothing is ever black and white. Most things are somewhere in the middle – grey – and there many, many shades of grey.

But what I really need to know is, does grey have colours in it? Real ones, like purple, yellow, green? I miss colours. A lot.

But you can't help me this time. If there's one thing I've learned, growing up, it's that there are times when you have to work stuff out for yourself. It's horrible. That's why I hang on to a friend who can help me a bit.

Maybe one day I'll tell you about him.

So, dear Estella. Thanks for listening.

Yes, I know, I know. Now that I'm growing up, I need to learn to sort some things out for myself.

Or, just find the right friends to help. What's that? There are signs? What signs?

OK, I promise I'll look out for them.

Can you stay a bit longer? Just until I fall asleep.

Goodnight, queen of the Amazons. Watch over the stars for me, dear Estella.

Mafalda

Click.

Things I've learned to do without my glasses that I really enjoy	My dreams for the future
Play the guitar	Be friends with Filippo forever
Listen to audiobooks	Fly on a plane to faraway places
Go to school (almost) by myself	Become a guitarist or writer
Run like the wind with my imagination	Just three dreams for now, I'll add more no doubt as I get older
Make pancakes	
Study (more darkness = better memory)	
Write a book using a computer that can turn what I say into writing and then read the writing back to me	

Today, the first of May, I, Mafalda, aged thirteen and a half, am getting married.

1

Dance With Us, Mafalda!

Dance with us, Mafalda!

I'm in a lush green meadow.

Sunlight is drenching everything in colour – the sky, the hills in the distance, the blossoming cherry tree in the middle of the meadow.

It feels so good to be running through the grass, not having to worry about tripping over! I'm as light as a feather, confident, and I feel like I'm flying. I can see ants, butterflies, tiny clouds swirling and blending into bigger ones, like whipped cream across an endless cloth of blue.

In my dreams I can see everything! I glance down at my shadow: I'm an eagle! I'm soaring on the wind. I'm happy, so happy I laugh with pure joy.

Mafalda! Come and join us!

Who's that calling me? A group of people dressed in big billowy clothes in a rainbow of colours are playing drums and flutes around the cherry tree, skipping to the beat of a music that's calling me to join them.

I glide over and feel myself turn back into Mafalda. All the girls and women I know are right there before me! Mum in a flowery headband, the girls in my class barefoot, Estella and Grandma leaping higher than everyone else to the music.

The cherry tree flutters its braids of blossom to the rhythm of the beating drums; it looks happy.

I'm coming!

I join the circle. The others smile and sing – we could stay like this forever. But I'm distracted by a *miaow* from above. I look up through the emerald-green leaves to see Ottimo Turcaret, my cat, only the younger, kitten version of him. He's stuck again. I make my way up the tree confidently, reach Ottimo and tuck him gently into my pocket. From up high I watch the others dance and wave to us. How beautiful life is! I laugh and rock gently on the branch.

A wooden door opens in the cherry-tree trunk below me and a girl I don't know steps out. She's playing a drum that's bigger than she is. I can't see her face because she's looking the other way, but even from behind, I can tell how strong and beautiful she is. She has long hair, swirling down her back, and red ribbons around her wrists, waist and ankles.

My friends fall in behind her. One by one, they walk away from the tree. 'Mafalda, come with us!' They form a tribe, marching as one behind the strong, beautiful girl. I want to go with them!

Wait for me!

I try to get down from the cherry tree. I know how to do it now, but the white clouds have turned grey and slid in front of the sun, leaving only darkness and a growing silence now that the group has gone. What's happening? What's going on? Why has everything turned so dark and ugly?

Even Ottimo Turcaret scrambles out of my pocket, down the tree and runs off into the distance.

Wait for me! I shout.

He stops for a second, looks back hesitantly, then vanishes, swallowed by the darkness.

High up in the tree, all I can see is a tiny red dot, far, far away now – the girl with the long hair. I wonder who she is and if I'll ever be as strong and beautiful as her.

The branch creaks and I realise there's someone else sitting on it now. 'Dad?'

It's him, I recognise the smell of his herbal shampoo. 'Dad?'

No reply.

I reach out to touch him but realise his weight has gone from the branch.

I wake up.

'DAD!!'

'What's up, Mafalda? Another nightmare?'

7

Mum comes into my room and opens the window. She doesn't pull up the blinds; there's no need of course, because the darkness will still be there, inside my eyes.

I try to calm down. 'Yes, but it's all right now. What time is it?'

Walking out into the hall she calls back to me, 'It's half past seven. You'd better hurry!'

I root around under the covers. I'm sure I had my voice recorder in my hand before I fell asleep last night. Ah, there it is.

Click.

Good morning. It's me again, Mafalda. I had another dream about the dancing girls last night. I wish I could be like their leader, but it's no use, I'm not like girls my age. I'm not even sure what girls my age are like, to be honest. I was younger when I ended up in the dark and of course they were younger then, too. Who knows how much they've grown, what they dress like now. They won't be like me for sure.

The worst thing about the dream was how it ended – me alone, up the tree, no Dad. Most children are afraid of the dark – they think it's the scariest thing in the world. Not me. With losing my sight I've learned there are no monsters in the dark, only shadows. Shadows of my parents, of my best friend Filippo, and of

*Ottimo Turcaret. If one of these shadows were
to disappear without a sound, now that would
be scary.*

'Mafalda, put that recorder away. You're going to
be late!'

I get up, pick up the trousers I left out last night for
school, put them on and stick the voice recorder into
my pocket. Dad gave me it ages ago and I absolutely
adore it. It's like keeping a diary, only easier for me to
use. I prefer things I can touch – feel the buttons under
my fingers, the click that tells me when to speak. I know
it's a bit old-fashioned but all the files I record would
never fit on my phone and, well, it was a present from
Dad. I love, love, love it.

T-shirt and sweater now. Oh, better close that window
first. It's January and freezing cold. I used to love January –
the middle of winter when the stars are brightest.

Oh, there's my favourite red sweater. I can be sure it's
red because red is the one remaining colour that can
get through the fog in my eyes.

I retrieve a trainer from under the bed and head into
the kitchen, feeling my way along the wall. Ottimo
Turcaret plays with the other one. We moved into
this new flat when my sight started to deteriorate and
Mum and Dad thought it would be easier to live close
to school. The kitchen and living room are in the same
room – open plan, they call it. I like it. When I'm sitting

at the kitchen table, the sun streams in from the balcony and warms my face, and I can hear the sound of my school across the road. Kids are already beginning to gather outside the gate and the hum they're making sounds like lightning crackling. I know what's behind the frisson – our mid-year report cards are being given out today! Secondary school is hard work. I might have to hide up the cherry tree again.

Oh, if only I could! I'm on the big-school side of the fence now, so even though I know the cherry tree is still there just a couple of metres away, only the primary kids get to enjoy it. I'm so jealous!

Jealousy. What a strange feeling. It smells like petrol, which I don't mind to be honest, but who wants to smell of petrol? I take my mug of hot milk out to the balcony.

'You'll catch your death out there!' Mum yells.

How annoying. I pretend not to hear and pull the French door shut behind me. Ooh, the kids waiting outside the school smell like popcorn today! Someone must've convinced their parents to take them to the cinema last night, as it was Sunday yesterday.

There was no point me asking. I can't watch films any more. I've tried following one without seeing the images but it's hard and it just makes me feel sad. From out here on the balcony, I can hear Mum and Dad talking in their bedroom – Dad spends nearly all his time in there these days.

'Are we managing?'

'More or less. You really need to find work, Giovanni.'

'There's nothing to be found.'

'But don't you have an interview tomorrow?' Mum's voice is trying to sound patient and hopeful.

'It was cancelled. The employment office should be calling me back next week about updating my CV.' Dad's voice sounds patient as well, only I can't detect any hope in it. I usually imagine words of hope, or just nice words in general, to be the colour blue. Dad's words have no colour.

'You've been saying that for six months now.'

'What else am I supposed to do? This is the way things are now and no magic wand's going to change it.'

'I know, but I think you should . . .'

I stop listening. Dad lost his job last summer. I feel guilty spending money at the cinema when we need it to pay the bills and rent. Bills and rent, bills and rent, that's all Mum ever talks about; oh, and money to buy food.

Prang!

The balcony railing vibrates in my hand. Ottimo must've leapt out of the kitchen too fast and forgot to stop. I nearly slosh the contents of my mug over him! He stretches out at my feet, rolling this way and that, bumping my shoes out of the way. 'Ottimo, that was quite an entrance. Are you all right?'

I force my feet into my shoes without untying the laces and go back inside. Mum's working her way around the table, clearing away the breakfast things, and bumps into me. I move out of the way (I've learned the layout of the flat by now), place my mug in the sink, turn the tap on to rinse it. Mum hates it when we leave the mugs and they go sticky on the bottom. I tell Mum I'm going to pop in and say goodbye to Dad.

'Good girl. Mafalda . . .'

'What?'

'I'll plait your hair if you want.'

'No thanks.'

'It won't take a minute.'

'No thanks.'

I hear her sigh and smile at the same time. She's the only person I know who can do that.

I escape down the hallway. If only she'd accept that I want to wear my hair down now – is it too much to ask?

I slow down when I reach my parents' bedroom. The darkness is much darker here, more than in the other rooms. I don't knock but go inside on my tiptoes.

'Dad?'

The sheets, pillow and mattress creak. Dad has rolled over in bed. I know sheets, pillows and mattresses don't creak, but to me it sounds like they're about to break because Dad has been in there so long. Even his voice creaks. 'What's up?'

I make my way over to the bed, not bumping anything. I know the position of every piece of furniture in this room: the chest of drawers, the wardrobe, the chair Mum

sits on to put on her pyj[...]
around me.

'I'm going to school, n[...]
'Mmm. Remember to [...]
I'd like to ask him if he [...]
to do the shopping like he [...]
if he'll make lunch and e[...]
going into school from t[...]
think of me when he hear[...]

'Bye darling! Be g[...]
hear the door cl[...]
also slipped o[...]
'Hey, so[...]
I kn[...]
hi[...]

A long, gentle whistle, like a string being pulled taut, tickles my ears. The secret whistle! Dad pats my hand on the bed, two quick taps. 'Off you go. And Mafalda . . .'

I turn back to face him from the doorway. 'I know, Dad. Don't worry. I won't forget to boogie-woogie.'

Click.

The boogie-woogie is our secret code for don't forget to enjoy yourself, give it your best shot. But also 'come back soon'. When I'm in bed at night, he'll come in to ask if I did the boogie-woogie and I nod, which means, 'Yes, everything's OK, I'm still here.' It's the only thing we say to each other all day.

It's late. I have to get a move on. A quick visit to the bathroom to wash my face, brush my teeth and have a wee. Then over to the door to pick up my rucksack, which is sitting packed and waiting for me. 'Bye everyone!'

good,' Mum says from behind me. I
ck shut at my back. I bet Ottimo has
t at the last minute. I knew it! There he is.
uishy, how's things?' a voice says.
ow it's Filippo waiting for me even before I hear
hollering or smell his honey-cornflake smell. It's
like his shadow comes to let me know. His shadow or
something like that. In my head I see Filippo crouched
down on the pavement and Ottimo Turcaret, tummy in
the air, enjoying having it rubbed. I make my way over
to join them at 'Mafalda speed', which is almost normal
now. I've learned that the entrance to our building leads
out into the lane which joins the road that goes to school,
but it's still really, really weird making my way around
in this dark grey fog. But, as Grandma used to say, you
get used to everything.

'Not those glasses again?' Filippo asks the minute he
sees me. We set off for school. He'd like to hold hands;
it's easier to lead me, he says, but I'm too embarrassed.
I'm embarrassed about my eyes, too. I've no idea what
they do, how they move, now that I'm in the dark. That's
why I prefer to keep glasses on. So I look like a girl who
needs glasses, nothing else.

'Yes, glasses again.'

'You don't need them. Why don't you leave them at
home?'

'And why do you keep leaving your head at home? It
might come in handy, you know.'

14

Filippo laughs and pats my arm, which means we need to cross the road, but there's someone walking past. He comes into the grounds of the big school with me. I catch the pitter patter of Ottimo's paws as he darts through all the pairs of feet to go and stretch out on the low branches of the cherry tree.

The cherry tree is still very special to me, even though I can't see it any more. I always think of Grandma and my dear friend Estella as living in it, inside the trunk I mean. For me, their souls are like bright, bright shadows, playing together inside the trunk, coming out at night to visit me in my dreams.

In front of the main entrance, I turn towards home, lift a hand and wave. You never know.

2

You Never Know

Good, we made it.

Filippo and I walk down to the end of the corridor on the left and arrive outside the door to my classroom. I trust him. We became really close friends last year . . . You could say he's my only friend, and I'm his. The only problem is he's not going to have much time to hang out with me from now on. He's in the year above me and has some big exams in June, so really needs to boogie-woogie. 'Sorry, Maf, they didn't fail me this year either,' he announces at the end of every school year. 'I'll have another go next year to see if we can get in the same class.'

'Shall I walk you to your desk?' he asks far too loudly, as always. I touch his arm (he has his hand in a fist, resting on his hip, a typical Filippo pose – also one of Estella's, my dearest, old friend). 'No thanks. I'll see you at break.'

'OK. I'll come to you,' he replies. Then he's gone, taking all my courage with him. I only say that because it takes nerves of steel to get through a day at big school. It's a bit like a jungle, full of wild animals. If Estella were here, she'd push me straight inside and help me get over my fears! She was one of my favourite caretakers who worked at the school and also a dear friend; she taught me how to be brave.

'No pain, no gain,' Grandma also used to say. I'm about to step inside the classroom when a voice gasps my name from further down the corridor. 'Mafalda, wait!'

I hover in the doorway to wait for Carola, my 'special needs' assistant. Can there be anything worse for someone my age at high school than being blind and very uncool? Yes, I'm afraid so. Having to have a special needs assistant.

'I searched the whole playground for you! You need to wait for me when you get here. I'll bring you in.'

Gosh. Carola stresses me so much I actually miss Fernando, the assistant I had at primary school. At least he used to ignore me and I could get on with things myself.

'Miss, I can cope by myself today.'

I have to at least try. It's embarrassing, although I realise she's only trying to help.

'What do you mean "by yourself"? Don't be silly. I'll help you take notes.'

'I'm allowed to record lessons,' I insist, pulling my amazing voice recorder out of my pocket. I can't record the lessons on my phone because we have so many periods every day.

'Oh, OK. Well, I'll help you with the essay. You dictate, I'll write.'

'I can do that on the computer. I hope they're not going to set a test the first day back after the Christmas holidays. Have you heard anything?'

I start to feel nervous and my mind goes straight back to the first day of secondary school. The bell had rung for the start of lessons, five minutes had gone by and the class was sitting in silence. I was sure everyone was looking at me. The only people I knew from primary school were Roly, Daniela and Mirko. But Mirko has never forgiven me for stealing his lunchbox when I ran away to the cherry tree and Daniela made friends on the first day with two girls I don't like, including one I really don't like called Debbie. The boys all talk about her at break – they think she's gorgeous. All I know is she ignores me and smells of jelly beans.

'Carola, come on inside. You can help someone else today. Come in, Mafalda.'

The teacher for our first period saves me. It's English – my favourite subject. And she's also my favourite teacher. She smells of vanilla and . . . newspaper ink. The same smell Dad used to have on his fingers on Sunday mornings when he read the papers.

'Miss, today's the day we change seats,' Daniela says as I sit down at my desk, stumbling just the once on someone's bag. At the start of every month we switch seats to sit beside someone new, so we can make friends, the teachers say. If you ask me, it doesn't work. I always end up sitting beside a boy who groans because he'd rather be beside his friends.

The teacher generally ignores the complaints and sits us where she wants. Today I end up with Debbie as desk-mate. Great. Now I have to put up with her jelly-bean smell for a whole month. I hear her giggling with the other girls as she comes over to sit beside me. I busy myself with my pencil case and jotter.

Click, snap.

Zip. Zap.

Bags and pencil cases open and shut. I listen to the sound of pens and pencils clacking against each other, pages ruffling. Chalk scrapes, screeches even, across the board, like a car braking.

'Well, class. Firstly, I'd like to announce that the book challenge is now officially open.'

I tap the triangle play button on my recorder. Click.

'As you all know, I want you to read as many books as you can from now to the end of the school year.'

'What, like books with words in?' Marco Valenti asks. He's always asking silly questions to try and make his friends laugh.

They laugh.

'Yes, Marco, like real books. Over the next few months, I'm challenging you to read as many as you can and write me a report for each whole book you finish, including a summary of the plot and descriptions of the characters.'

'Is there a prize? I'm not doing anything unless there's a prize!' Marco says. More laughing.

'Marco Valenti, if you have something to say, raise your hand please. Anyway, the answer is no, there are no prizes, but you'll get an extra point in your file for each book read. Five points will raise your end-of-term mark by ten per cent.'

'So, does that mean if I have fifty per cent for Maths in June, but I read five books, you'll give me sixty per cent?'

'Yes, that's it exactly. Worth a try, don't you think?'

Hmm. This sounds interesting. Not so much for the marks but to see who reads the most books.

'How will you do it?' Debbie whispers to me under her breath.

'Do what?'

'Read.'

'I listen to audiobooks.'

'Miss, can we listen to audiobooks as well?'

What is her problem?

I bet the teacher's looking straight at us.

'Anyone who can read from printed books has no need to use an audiobook,' she says.

Debbie insists, 'But that's not fair! She'll get through the books quicker than us.'

That 'she' is me.

'Deborah, everyone will proceed at their own speed. Mafalda will have to hand in book reports like everyone else. I don't want any copying and you are not permitted to get an adult to write them for you. I will be able to tell!'

'What's your problem?' I hiss through my teeth at Debbie.

'Me? I don't have a problem.'

Yeah, right. I grip the recorder tighter and go back to listening to the teacher. I know what anger smells like now. Burnt jelly beans.

I always think the first break on the first day back at school is depressing. Instead of taking it easy, all you can think about is how far away June feels while watching all the stupid little cliques forming.

Thank goodness I have Filippo.

'Mafalda, shall we go outside and play at something?'

Poor Carola. 'Play at something' means she can't think of anything suitable for someone who can't see.

'Thanks, Miss, but I'm waiting for a friend.' Thankfully I hear Filippo hollering at the classroom door. 'Hey, aren't you coming? I brought a banana – what have you got?'

I take my snack out of the front pocket of my bag and walk as politely as possible around the dark shadow that is Carola. 'I made a sandwich with olives.'

'Superb! Shall we split it?'

We go into the corridor and head down the stairs to go outside. Filippo is one step ahead of me, just in case. My heart fluttered a little when we went past the caretakers' room. It's not the room Estella used to have but the smell's the same – coffee and printer ink. Oh, and glass cleaner that smells pretty much identical to the one she used.

We walk along the fence, Filippo munching on my sandwich – no doubt he'll leave me a few crumbs – and I eat his banana while thinking about my sandwich.

'Why did *you* make this?' he asks. 'Did your mum forget? That's not like her.'

'No, she didn't forget. I'm just trying to do things myself these days.'

'Why?'

Filippo is magical. Magical and irritating – he always notices when something's up, ignores the fact that you might not want to talk about it and keeps on at you until he finds out what's going on.

'No reason. You know I'm trying to do things myself these days.' I try to dodge the question.

'Why these days in particular?'

'Well, I just don't want to cause any more hassle at home, OK?'

'Hassle for who?'

'Mum.'

'Why?' he insists, handing me back the tinfoil my sandwich was wrapped in. It feels pretty much empty.

'Filippo, making things difficult for your mum might seem normal to you. But not for me.'

His anything-but-reassured shadow moves away a little. I hear him kick a football (followed by a collective yell from the kids who were playing with it – he must've kicked it miles away) then he's back. He plants himself in front of my face. I miss seeing his dimples. I'd like to caress his face, feel the little depressions in his cheeks, but how embarrassing that would be with the whole school looking on!

'You said any *more* hassle. Why, what other problems are there?'

I press my face between the railings of the fence and grip the metal bars tight with my hands. The chill of the cold metal feels good on my skin.

'You know Dad's not working . . .'

'Yeah, but what about it? He'll find something else.'

I sigh, heavy-hearted. 'If he got out of bed!'

We sit on the wall. The mayhem of school break lifts my hair, like a gentle gust of wind. The rest of the world always seems miles away, a distant darkness, when I'm talking to Filippo; together, things are much less scary.

'How long has he been in bed for?'

'Since his firm closed down.'

'That was six months ago!'

'I know.'

'We need to do something. Find him a job.'

23

I laugh, although I want to cry. 'It's not that easy, you know. It's not like waving a magic wand.'

'Well, if you start with an attitude like that . . .'

He's right. I'm feeling too sad to think about this seriously.

'Listen, I have an idea,' he announces. 'Have someone bring you round to mine on Saturday. We'll get a pizza and make a plan.'

'A plan. Good. But enough of that for now. Let's talk about our report cards. Are you going to do some home study or not?'

'Eugh, Mafalda. It's so boring. Did I tell you my English teacher has given me a ton of books to read?'

The bell rings and we head back to the stairs to go inside. 'I've got loads, too. We can swap if you like. Maybe you can even help me read them?'

'In your dreams! But I'm OK for the swap though.'

I give him as firm a pat on the arm as I can. We pass under the branches of the cherry tree which overhang our part of the school grounds. In my head I'm saying 'Hi!' to the giant, to Grandma and to Estella. I bet they're playing chess in there while I'm having to manage on my own out here. It's so unfair.

Back in class, Debbie speaks to me the minute we take our seats. Weird.

'Can I ask you something?'

'Erm . . .'

24

'What's wrong with your eyes?'

I turn my face towards her, but only fleetingly. I know some people feel uncomfortable when I look straight at them and I was pretty sure no one would see my fog if I kept it hidden behind my glasses. 'I have a disease which causes spots to form in my eyes and they've grown so big I can't see any more.'

'You can't see anything?'

'Just shadows, and the colour red. But I can hear and smell just fine. They're going to cure me. Very soon.'

'Wow, really?'

'Yes.'

I don't know why I said that. There *is* no cure for my eyes – the doctor told me that last time I went to see her.

It's probably really stupid, but I want Debbie to like me. Maybe I should try talking to her. She might wear glasses as well, or have something else going on with her.

'So what problem do you have?'

Silence.

'There's nothing wrong with me,' Debbie finally replies then turns towards the teacher who has just come in.

Yeah right, nothing wrong. They all say that.

Brrrring!!!!

Alarm clock.

Isn't it Saturday today? I must've forgotten to turn it off. Pity. I was dreaming about the dancing girls and the girl with the long hair.

'Morning, squishy.'

Ottimo is lying on my tummy and I bet he gave me one of his looks when the alarm went off. He's not the type of cat to jump on you in the morning to wake you up. He would happily sleep until lunchtime on the weekend.

'Let's go have breakfast,' I suggest, throwing off the covers. Nothing doing. Ottimo slides sideways without altering position. I hear him continue to snore so decide to leave him in peace.

Click.

Mafalda here. I'm starting to obsess that if I can't get a job when I grow up, I'll disappear. Like disappear and die. I'm not sure what I can and can't dream for when I'm big . . . My eyes don't work so my dreams are obviously going to be a bit different from everyone else's. I'm meeting Filippo this evening. I'll ask him what he thinks I can do.

The quiet of a Saturday morning in January has the chirping of baby birds in it and the flimsiest of sunrays peeking through half-lowered blinds. I go into the kitchen and hear the sound of the moka pot being lifted then lowered. Mum's up and about already. Good. The smell of coffee brewing in the morning makes me feel happy, the one time in the day I'm the same as everyone else. It comforts me to think that, in every home of everyone I know, there'll be someone in the kitchen making coffee just like in our home.

I decide to ask Mum if we can do something together today.

'Sorry darling, I have work.'

I flop onto a chair. 'On a Saturday? You're usually off at the weekend.'

'Since the start of the new year I have to work Saturdays as well, but just until three p.m. I told you. Maybe we can do something when I get home.'

I blow on my mug of hot milk. She always heats it up too much. By three o'clock in the afternoon she'll be tired and will still have the shopping to do, so we won't be going anywhere. I'd like to ask if I can invite Filippo over but I don't want to disturb Dad. I'd better just go over to Filippo's house.

Plates clatter into the dishwasher. I take my chance while Mum's back is turned. Where's the moka pot? She usually leaves it in the middle of the table. I reach out, cautiously – I don't want to scald my fingers. I find the handle and pour some coffee into my milk.

'Oh no.'

'What's up?' Maybe she spotted me. She thinks I'm still too young for coffee.

'We're out of sugar. I'll pop upstairs and ask if our neighbour's got any.'

I spring to my feet. 'I'll go.'

Mum says nothing for a second or two. I know she's still scared of me using the stairs in the dark. That's why we got a ground floor flat. Before she can say anything, I nip out and go up the stairs.

It's actually quite easy: steps are steps, as long as you keep putting one foot in front of the other, raising them just enough each time so you don't trip. Just to be sure, though, I count them. It's the first time I've come upstairs since we moved here.

Six, seven, eight, nine . . .

There are fourteen steps between our flat and Mr . . . erm, what's our upstairs neighbour called? Mr Rossi, I think. Mum always says hello to him. She calls him by his first name, Nino, when she sees him out on his balcony (where he seems to spend most of the time). He likes to watch people coming in and out, right above our flat. He hardly ever leaves his flat though. And he doesn't make much noise. He must be old.

I've been here for two years and have never spoken to him apart from one time he shouted 'young lady' at me from his window and asked me if my cat was allergic to anything. 'Pollen,' I replied without thinking. Mr Rossi slammed the window shut again. I realised he must've been referring to when Ottimo Turcaret slinks up the stairs to his flat looking for treats, and he wanted to know if he had any food allergies.

Now comes the hard part. Where's the door? In the same place as our door, I imagine. Let's hope there are no flowerpots or rugs on the landing. I take a few steps to the left. Great, there's the handle. That was easy.

I could try to find the bell but knocking is simpler. I knock. And wait. And wait some more. After what feels like ages, *creak!*, the door opens. Mr Rossi's there, bringing with him the smell of minestrone soup and air freshener.

'Er, hello. Could we borrow some sugar?'

'Hello, aren't you the girl from downstairs? The owner of the cat that comes to visit me?' I think his voice sounds a bit abrupt at first but deep, deep down I can detect the same cushion of kindness I think all old people have in their voices.

'Yes, that's me.'

'Well, I'm afraid I don't have any sugar. I'm diabetic.'

Hmm, I wonder what that means.

'But I have some sweetener if that's any use.'

I have no idea what sweetener is but, for fear of offending Mr Rossi, I say yes and hear his steps retreat – slowly and a little heavily if I have to be honest – a door opening, a cup clanging on a counter then steps coming back towards me.

'Here you are.'

He's probably holding out the cup to me. Does he know I can't see? Not many people notice at first because I like to keep my eyes open (when it gets too much, I occasionally give in and close them, even when there are other people there) and I also try to walk normally, not slowly or hesitantly. It's sometimes a bit scary but I hate people to notice right away that I'm in the dark.

Right now I'm not sure what to do. While I hum and haw, the cup is put into my hands and the door to Mr Rossi's flat shuts in my face. 'Thanks,' I say to the door.

As I start back down the stairs, it feels like I have two headlights boring into my back, or two sticks, like the ones old people use to get around, only these ones are being poked between my shoulder blades. I imagine Mr Rossi has opened the door again to check I've gone. Before I turn the corner to start down another flight of stairs, I raise a hand and wave. You never know.

3

A Talented Chef and Expert Bike Fixer

Afternoon, in the garden, bored.

I wonder what the other girls in my class are doing. They'll be at the shopping centre buying clothes or at the hairdresser. I twiddle a lock of my hair. It's grown really long and has knots at the ends. I should probably go to the hairdresser too.

What silly thoughts. When I get these kinds of thoughts, there's a special place I like to hide.

I walk across the grass without touching the railings or the fence behind the communal shed where the residents of our building keep the lawnmower, rakes and other gardening tools. Here it is, my secret hiding place. The shed is a proper log cabin with a wooden door and two tiny square windows criss-crossed with strips of wood, which are full of splinters. I know this because I explored every corner of the place when we moved here. I like spending time by myself in the garden shed: it's not that different from being outside to be honest, and there's a lovely smell of cut grass.

Click.

Mafalda here, from the garden shed. There's one thing I definitely want to do at some point, and that's fly. It must be weird getting on a plane without seeing anything, maybe not realising when it's taking off, or even being scared by this. But my mind keeps going back to the green meadow in my dream. I have a feeling it's somewhere far, far away. One day I'd like to go there and run through it.

Cherry tree, I know you can't answer because you're a tree but maybe you can hear me. I'm at the window of the garden shed and I know you're there, by the school, all alone like me. Mum is busy doing non-stop washing loads. Dad's in his room, sleeping, or thinking about his tiny office at the building site that he can't go to any more, who knows.

If you're looking for something to do today, darling tree, send me some luck on a leaf. My heart wobbles whenever I think about getting on a plane for the first time; a bit like when I thought I was in love with Filippo. I get the

feeling these things are complicated, which is
why I need your help.

. . .

I'm standing by the bathroom door, waiting for the right moment to speak to Mum, inhaling the scent of the washing machine, the door just opened at the end of a cycle.

'Mum.'

'What?'

She must be bent over the machine. I hear the sound of tugging as she hauls the clean clothes out of the drum.

'Can you take me to Filippo's house tonight?'

'OK. I don't want you two going out, though.'

'No, we won't.'

What she doesn't know is that we've been going out to the local pizza shop on our own for the past six months! If everyone else our age can go, why shouldn't we?

Mum walks past me, puffing, carrying the red laundry basket, which I bet is piled high. She only has time to get through it all at the weekend.

I follow her out onto the balcony. The clothes horse clacks metallically on the tiles. I stop at the door, my back against the French window which is damp with condensation because it's so cold outside.

'Listen . . .'

'What? Hand me the peg basket, will you? It's right there – if you bend over you'll feel it.'

'OK. Listen, since I'm going to Filippo's, can we make

33

a cake to take with me? His mum always makes us one when I'm there.'

To be honest, it's just an excuse so Mum and I can do something together.

'There's a boxed jam tart in the cupboard. You can take that.'

'But that's not a proper cake. I meant a home-made one, like a sponge or something.'

Mum continues hanging up clothes. 'Mafalda, I have too much to do. I still need to clean the bathroom, change the beds, do the ironing then . . . Oh heck, I also forgot to pay the water bill. I must remember to go there on Monday, that way I can pop into the car insurance company as well. And don't forget you have a dental appointment on Wednesday.'

'What, for braces?'

'Yes.'

'I don't want braces.'

'If the dentist says you need braces, then you get braces.'

'What a pain.'

'Take your dad his coffee, will you.'

She goes inside and disappears back into the bathroom.

My glasses slide down my nose. I nudge them up. She can forget me ever putting braces on my teeth. Not going to happen. I swear I'll lock myself in the garden shed all winter if they try to force me.

There's a red tray on the worktop. I pick it up and put

a coffee cup already filled with coffee on it. It almost tips over but I save it in time.

I take Dad his food on a Saturday, but it doesn't mean we speak any more than usual. I feel bad because instead of spending time with him, sometimes I ride on the back of Filippo's bike to get ice cream or stay out of the way in my room or in the garden shed.

I go into Mum and Dad's room where the darkness is much darker. Today a heavy smell of memories hangs in the air. I couldn't say exactly what they smell of. Maybe good memories smell a bit like talcum powder, although I probably only think that because Grandma used it all the time. Really sad memories smell of over-ripe fruit. All memories make your eyes and nose sting after a few minutes though, so best not to smell them too long.

'What are you doing, Dad?'

I hear the sound of plastic, a box lid being laid down somewhere, maybe on the chest of drawers. Dad sighs and even that cracks the air like ice when you walk on it.

'Nothing. I was just looking at old photos.'

I go over to him. He takes the tray from me and lays it on the bed on Mum's side. I sit down beside him.

'Who of?'

'Oh, just photos I took years ago with the guys at work. We were all up in the mountains together in this one. Do you remember? The time we went to the Dolomites. Livio was there with his kids. Remember?'

I can't see the photo he's holding but I know exactly

which one it is. We had so much fun that time with his workmates, especially Livio, who made us all laugh, and his daughter – Emma I think her name was; she was really nice.

But that was years ago.

Dad's workmates came to see him a couple of times after he got the sack. He still talks to Livio on the phone. Two of the others ended up without a job after the company went bust; everyone else was found a new position. Or so Dad says. He was sacked because he was the youngest, apparently.

'How long did you work there, Dad?'

I know he likes to talk about his work.

'Since before you were born. It was my first real job, you know. I was so proud. I came home with the signed contract and your grandparents cracked opened a bottle of bubbly to celebrate, then Mum and I started looking for a house.'

'And you got married.'

'Yes. All my workmates came to the wedding. There has to be a group photo here somewhere.'

I hear him rummaging under the sheets. He must have photos all over the bed.

'Dad . . .'

'Yes? Where's that wedding photo got to?'

'Do you ever think about getting a new job?'

He doesn't reply. Just feels around a bit more, then stops. 'Here it is! Aw, isn't it magnificent? We were all so young, and look at Teo – he still had hair back then!'

He laughs. But it's not a pretty sound. Dad normally has a beautiful laugh. He doesn't use it much but when he does, it's infectious – it makes everyone start laughing. Like a thunderclap, or a stormy sky breaking out a smile.

The laugh I heard just now was more like a raindrop falling from the gutter and creeping down the back of your neck.

'Dad . . .'

'Mmm?'

'Can we make a cake together?'

'A cake? I don't know how.'

'We could try. You used to like cooking.'

Silence. For a fleeting second it feels like he might be contemplating it. The mattress bounces beneath me. Could he be getting up? 'Come on, Dad.'

'I'm not in the mood, Mafalda. Lower the blinds on your way out, will you? Thanks.'

The pizza parlour we normally go to is not far along the road from Filippo's house – just thirty-four steps. It's seven o'clock in the evening and it's already very dark. One of the things I miss the most is seeing the steam puff out of people's mouths when it's freezing cold outside.

We walk quickly. The pizza shop will be nice and warm when we get inside.

'OK, so I spoke to Mum and she says we need to spread the word.'

I rub my gloved hands together. Brrr.

'What, about a job for Dad you mean?'

'Yes. We need to tell people, look online.'

'Maybe we could post an ad?'

'Good idea. Mind the step.'

He still warns me even though I've learned there's a step. Filippo throws open the door to the pizza parlour and I'm immediately wrapped in the buzz of the place and the cornucopia of delicious odours.

'Is there anyone from my class?' I ask.

'Hmm. Yes. Roly. A couple of your friends. And the pretty one.'

Debbie. I don't feel like saying hello to her. And I don't like hearing him call her 'the pretty one' either.

'They're not my friends.'

'Don't say that. Take a seat here and I'll go and order.'

While I'm waiting, I look for a napkin to wipe one of the taller counters we like to sit at. It's always sticky.

'Mafalda?'

Daniela. She must be here with the others.

'*Ciao.*'

'*Ciao.*'

'Are you here with Filippo from the year above?'

'Yeah, why?'

I hear her giggle with her head half-turned to look behind her. Amid the commotion of the pizza parlour, I also hear the other girls in my class giggling. They must be sitting in the opposite corner.

'Listen, a friend of mine wants to know if he's your boyfriend.'

'Who, Filippo?'

'Yeah.'

'No, we're friends; best friends,' I add.

'Ah, OK, thanks.' She walks away.

Filippo returns with our pizzas and two glasses of Coke. He lays it all out on the narrow counter and clambers up on the stool beside mine. Sitting like this, we both have our backs to the rest of the room. The girl on the till shouts out the numbers of people queuing for takeaways when their pizzas are ready.

'Filippo, someone's got their eye on you.'

'What?' he mumbles, mouth full of pizza.

'One of the girls in my class came and asked me if you're single.'

I can't tell him what she actually asked. He'd laugh in my face.

'And what did you say?'

'That you're single.'

'Who was it?'

'Daniela asked me, but it was for one of her friends.'

'Which one?' he asks, his voice now coming from behind me. He must've twisted around to have a look.

'How do I know? Turn back round, will you!'

Everyone knows you don't turn around when you're talking about someone. Oh, there's that petrol-like smell again. I wonder where it's coming from? Must be a burnt pizza or something. But Filippo is already thinking about something else.

'Listen, grab a napkin and we'll write that ad for your dad. Have you got a pen? How about . . .

Giovanni, 39 years old, 1.8m tall, one daughter.
Experienced labourer and site supervisor.
Excellent computer skills.
Expert bicycle repairer, talented cook.
Good team worker.
Fluent in Italian, good written English,
intermediate French.
Seeks work locally. Serious and hardworking.

'Great,' he goes on. 'We'll put one up here in the pizza parlour, on the wall. Just let me take a photo of it on my phone.'

'Don't you think it sounds a bit weird?'

'What do you mean weird?'

'Well, it's not like the normal ads you see in the newspaper.'

Filippo stops. Maybe he's re-reading it. He takes ages.

'Listen, everyone puts their personal information, experience and language skills. It's fine.'

The truth is I'm not a hundred per cent convinced. We left his surname out of the personal information – I didn't want to invade Dad's privacy and I didn't put his phone number either. I used my own. Fingers crossed . . .

'How much do I owe you for the pizza?'

We go out into the cold, no doubt the eyes of my classmates all on our backs.

'Five euros.'

I take the money out of my pocket. 'Here. Mum gave me ten, but it's to last me all week, next weekend included.'

'Lucky you. My mum only gave me five. If I want any more I have to hoover and take the rubbish out.'

'OK, so . . . how much did you earn in total this week?'

'Five euros.'

This brings a smile to my face. We're walking back to Filippo's house when he suddenly stops, tightening his hand around my wrist. My heart does the weird fluttery thing again.

'Did you see that?'

'What?'

'The weird hippy woman. She's over there beside the bins with her dog. She sleeps on a piece of cardboard. Do you know the one I'm talking about?'

The hippy woman he's talking about lives rough and plays a flute made of lots of pipes with some other people who also live on the street. I've never seen her but I always stop and listen to them when I come into town with Mum. Dad used to give me coins to put in the guitar case they'd leave open on the ground, but he doesn't come to town with us any more.

'What does she look like?' I ask him.

'She has long hair that reaches right down her back,

an enormous smile and whenever I see her, she's always wearing big, baggy clothes. She plays loads of different instruments. Oh, she's seen us looking at her. Let's go!'

We set off again at a fast pace and pretty much hide in Filippo's doorway. As he shuts the door, I glance over in the direction of the bins and hear the hippy lady's dog give a soft whine. Maybe he's dreaming about running.

'Hey Filippo. Maybe you and I should find a job as well. You could hoover more and take out the rubbish. What can I do?'

'Hmm, I'll need to think about that and get back to you. It's not like you have the broadest of skill sets, eh?'

'There has to be something I can do!'

'Well, there is one. Singing. We could busk like those musicians. You sing, I'll play.'

'I'll think about it. Thanks for the advice.'

4

Time to Get Into Training

Click.

A life lived in fear is not a life. A life lived in fear
is not a life.

'What's up?'

Debbie. Desk next to mine. I can tell from her voice
when she's giving me daggers. If there's one thing I like
about her, just the one mind you, it's that she can't hide
that she doesn't like you. The usual sleepy, eight-o'clock-
in-the-morning murmur continues around us.

'Nothing's up. I'm just nervous about the geometry
test.'

'Why do you keep speaking into that thing?'

'It's a voice recorder.'

'If you say so.'

I bet she turned to her friends and face-palmed. *What a weirdo.* No one laughs, though. The teacher has come in and the smell of fear – wilted flowers and deodorant – spreads through the room.

'Do you know what you need to do to get over your nerves? Play the guitar,' Filippo would say.

Since we've been friends, we've been playing at his house at least once a week. Me on the guitar (I've learned to play quite well) and Filippo on the piano. We don't do proper songs – I can't read the music and I don't really have much of an ear. One day we just played the first thing that came to us, not bothering if it was in tune, the main thing being to have fun, and we've been doing it ever since. Filippo's mum heard us once and said we sounded like a pair of drunks who come to blows then make up again.

Filippo is never nervous before class tests because he always copies someone else. Oh, on the subject of copying . . .

'Psst.'

Is that Debbie calling me? The teacher has given out the test papers and Carola and I read through it together before she popped outside to make a photocopy.

'Hey Mafalda, are you deaf?' Her voice pierces the air like a snapped pencil.

'What do you want?' I hiss under my breath so the teacher won't hear.

'What's the formula for a circle?'

'Which part? Circumference or diameter?'

'You tell me – I don't know. Which one is it in question one?'

'Area. The radius squared multiplied by three point one four.'

'How do I work out the radius?'

'You have to –'

'Quiet over there! Mafalda, young lady, what do you think you're doing?'

No doubt my face has turned traffic light red.

'Miss, it's my fault. Honestly. I was just giving Mafalda a hand,' Debbie pipes up, certainly not to do me any favours. We're not allowed to ask our neighbours for help during a test. It's against the rules.

'Mafalda, if you have a question, please ask me. No asking a neighbour.'

I'm so angry I can't even splutter out the required 'Yes, Miss.' I'll get you back for that, Debbie.

Carola comes back in and I almost don't get through the test. I can't concentrate. By my side, Debbie eavesdrops on everything we say and I more or less end up doing the test for her.

We have double history for the next two periods and I don't hear any of it. Then it's English. The reading competition! I've been so preoccupied with finding Dad a job and my own stuff that I completely forgot about it. At break I give Filippo the list of books the teacher assigned us. 'Have you read any of them?'

'Snack bar please.'

Filippo and I have an agreement that when we like what the other one's having for lunch, we can ask to swap. I hand over my snack bar and my cereal yogurt.

'Tasty. No spoon?'

Filippo can be disgusting sometimes. 'If I give you my spoon, how do I eat my part? I don't want your saliva all over my spoon.'

'Ah, OK. Look, this is for you.' He hands me a packet of crackers and a fruit juice. At least the crackers are pizza-flavoured.

'Leave me some juice, will you? And a cracker.'

We're outside. I pull my beanie hat, no pom-poms, down over my ears. From the scoffing noises I'm hearing, Filippo has made a start on the snack bar already. 'Filippo, are you listening to me? Look at the list of books. I'm behind already.'

'Me too.'

I decide to prod a bit more. 'What have you got for me?'

Paper rustles. He's reading the list. Slowly. Very slowly. 'So?'

'Hang on a sec. Hmm, if you want I can tell you about *Jonathan Livingston Seagull*. That's about it, though.'

'Better than nothing. What do you have to read?'

'That book about the boy who runs away to live in trees.'

'*The Baron in the Trees*!'

'That's the one. Have you read it? Oh, and there's *The Little Prince*. And *Frankenstein*.'

'You're in luck! I've read two of those,' I exclaim. 'But you're on your own with *Frankenstein*. Are you sure you haven't read *Great Expectations*? Ever heard about it at school?'

'Nup, 'fraid not, beautiful.'

What an idiot – but I absolutely adore him. I wonder if he really thinks I'm beautiful. I haven't seen myself in the mirror for two years. I'd like to know if I look different, changed. I'm about to ask him when the bell rings.

I walk Filippo to his classroom. I don't feel like going straight back to mine and having Debbie's jelly-bean smell under my nose again.

'Any juice left?' he asks.

I hand over the carton. Noisily he sucks up what's left through the straw and . . . Plop! . . . lobs it straight into the bin as usual. 'Score!'

'Filippo, really?'

Uh-oh. That's the maths teacher's voice.

'What's up?' he asks.

'You have splashed juice everywhere. Look at the cabinet!'

'Miss, I'll get some paper and wipe it off.'

'You certainly will, then straight back for your test!'

Poor Filippo. Doing homework together, I realised that he's really talented at sums. But only in his head, because when he tries to write them down, it all goes wrong. This week he's studying the cartesian plane and absolutely hates it.

'It's like moving around a darkened room for me, with nothing to guide me. I just keep bumping into walls,' he told me yesterday. My heart started thumping like the drums of the dancing girls in my dream, even though I felt bad for him.

'You just back from seeing your boyfriend?' Debbie asks when I sit down.

'He's not my boyfriend.'

'Are you inviting him to your birthday party?'

How does she know when my birthday is? I hear her put something down on my desk. I reach out. It's my diary.

'Don't read my diary.'

'It's just a school diary, it's hardly private, is it? Anyway, I noticed that it's your thirteenth birthday next month. You not having a party?'

Debbie had an amazing pool party in July, just her and her closest friends. Filippo and I happened to be cycling past the front gates to her house and heard them splashing around. We couldn't see anything through the tall hedges.

'Of course I'm having a party.'

'Can I come?'

How do I say no, to her face? I don't know if Mum will let me invite everyone from the class. Our flat isn't big enough. And with Dad like he is . . .

Even worse . . . I've no idea if they'll even let me have a party! They can't afford it – they'd have to buy a cake, balloons, drinks and all the rest.

'Eh? OK.'

Lucky for me the PE teacher arrives. In six weeks' time we have a cross-country race behind the school. I pick up my gym bag. Time to get into training.

The corridor to the PE block goes past Filippo's classroom. The door is wide open. I can hear the craft and technology teacher explaining electrical circuits. Filippo is sitting at the back by the window. I know he'll see me go past, even briefly, so I wave.

What if the others are right and we're more than friends? Do I want us to be more than friends? And if I did, how would I tell him? Is it even up to me to make the first move? Or should I wait for him to?

Obviously I think all this silently to myself. I would never say it out loud, not even to the voice recorder. I'd be too scared Ottimo Turcaret might jump on it later, while there are people about, press 'Play' by mistake with his paw, and everyone would hear. No, no, no! I'd die of shame and have to run away to the cherry tree again. Forever this time.

We get to the changing rooms. The people in my class are buzzing about the cross-country race. I wish I could take part, on my own I mean, like everyone else, not with Carola, the special needs assistant, guiding me and – no disrespect to her – slowing me down. So I'll be staying on the sidelines to start the race, take times, do silly exercises like jumping on the spot. Then someone will take me up to the stand to cheer everyone on. How depressing.

I'm tying my shoelaces when Debbie speaks to me for the third time since the start of term. Her voice has a moderately kind ring to it, I'll give her that, but, for some reason I can't quite fathom, I smell trouble.

'Mafalda, can I tell the others?'

I raise my eyes to hers. 'Tell them what?'

I hear her turn to address everyone in the changing room. 'Mafalda's having a party for her birthday!'

Much cheering and clapping. Inside me, rage whistles like the steam on a pressure cooker.

'To be honest, I haven't given it much thought.'

'Oh, go on, you told me in class earlier! You said you were inviting everyone.'

I stand up and step closer to her. Much closer. I want my face to be right in hers, almost touching. Like when two people argue in films. 'I didn't ask for your help.'

A hush falls over the room.

'What are you getting so worked up about? Look, we'll all come to your party. It doesn't matter if your house is tiny . . .'

I give her an almighty shove backwards.

She doesn't fall. I hear her steps coming back towards me, angry. Don't cover your face with your hands,

50

Mafalda, don't do it, be brave! The shove she gives me takes me by surprise. I fall backwards and hit the coat hooks on the wall.

It's true that sometimes I just lose it. Everything goes dark red and I get a low rumble in my ears like engines revving. It scares me but I only realise it's happening after it's over. After I've caused the havoc I'm about to cause now.

I pick myself up and leap forward, aiming for where I think Debbie's hair is. From that moment it's all pulling, grabbing, scratching, rolling around on the dusty changing-room floor and a lot of cheering and chanting from the others, not to mention grunting from me and Debbie. Oh, and a couple of slaps are thrown in as well. Mine misses, hers doesn't.

'Stop that now!' Carola thunders as she rushes in. 'Everyone out! Mafalda, Deborah, on your feet.'

I hear the others slowly file out of the changing room.

I bet you're wondering how it all ended. Let me tell you! It ended in the principal's office. If Estella had been here, she would've said, 'See Mafalda? You still good at hit stupid girl even when eyes not work.' And she'd have been pleased. But Estella wouldn't have to go home and face her mum with a disciplinary letter from school. It's Mum who checks all my school stuff these days, my report cards, test results, all that kind of thing. They used to do it together, Mum and Dad, but I don't think Dad can be bothered any more. He doesn't seem to have much energy – he's always so tired.

After the visit to the principal I still had to go back to the sports field.

The voices of my classmates reach me from a distance. They're running.

'Are you mad at me, Carola?'

It's the first time I've ever used a teacher's first name. Carola sits down beside me on the first row of the stands, the one closest to the track.

'No. I just hate fighting. Especially between girls. Women shouldn't lower themselves that way.'

I'm not sure I understand, but I nod anyway. I'll think more about it later and decide if she's right or not. If you ask me, girls should be able to fight the same way boys can, although they can't go claiming to be superior afterwards.

'Listen Carola. I don't feel like jumping on the spot. Or cheering for the others.'

'What would you like to do then?' she asks, standing up.

'I want to run. On the track.'

Silence. Then her voice smiles, 'Yes, I think we could at least try.'

If we don't try, we'll never know, will we?

It's four o'clock on Tuesday afternoon, which means one thing and one thing only: lemon tea at Filippo's house. And music.

Filippo's mum Cristina invited me two years ago and said we should make a *ritual* out of it. That really

52

appealed to me because it reminded me of when Estella and I used to get together in her room to read *The Little Prince* in secret and talk about the tamed fox. I send Filippo an audio message.

Can you come round to mine today? I have tons of history homework.

He replies straight away.

OK.

Filippo was in fits of laughter when I told him about the fight with Debbie. 'Welcome to the club!' he said. I wasn't sure if he was referring to the fight club or being marched to the principal's office afterwards.

Debbie was there, too; the principal told her that it's wrong to hit people, especially people who have difficulties. Incidentally, the head also said she was especially angry with me because she would never have expected someone *like me* to lower herself to such behaviour, namely hitting a fellow pupil. What did she mean by that, someone *like me*? Is fighting off limits for girls and blind people? Looking back, what was the actual point of writing a list of things I can do without my eyes if there's all this extra stuff I *can't* do?

Bah. While I'm waiting for Filippo, I head for my parents' bedroom. Very slowly, just like always, I push open the door and breathe in. There's the smell of Mum's perfume (she always uses the one Cristina gave her last year) then the smell of Dad's silence, all hissy and crackly. He's still in bed.

'Dad?'

'Yeah?'

He sounds exhausted.

I take a step into the room, lay my hand on the chest of drawers, feel a picture frame. It's not the silver one with their wedding photo, but the wooden one with Grandma Alba inside.

'Dad, how did Grandma and Grandpa meet?'

Dad has always talked quite happily about his mum, never his dad.

'Not again.'

'Why?'

'Because your grandpa and I didn't get along. He was very strict.'

'What did he do?'

'He was a surveyor.'

'Did he build houses like you?'

'Yes, but he was much more talented. I'm just a site manager. And he was never fired.'

I move closer to the bed. 'But it wasn't your fault, Dad.'

He turns in the bed. 'I don't want to talk about it now.'

We remain in silence for a bit.

'Do you want to come out for a bike ride on Saturday?'

Dad loves cycling. He taught me how to ride without stabilisers when I was just two years old. With Dad holding on to me it was easy.

'Bikes? Where do you want to go?'

'Anywhere, wherever we want.'

Dad sighs. He won't say yes. I should've thought of somewhere specific to go before I asked him. At least I tried. If you don't try you'll never know, right?

Click.

Dearest cherry tree, send me a little luck: I need it for Dad this time. I can sense he'd like to run away and hide in your branches like I did last year, but I don't know if adults can do that. The thought of it makes me laugh, imagining my big, strong Dad perched on a branch eating cherries all day. But then I want to cry when I imagine him sad and alone up there.

My darling tree, how can I get this sad image out of my head? Send me a sign please.

5

Why Don't You Finish It?

Saturday afternoon again.

Filippo printed off some leaflets with the job advert for Dad at his mum's copy shop. We decided to pursue every option open to us.

We start handing them out in the area around Filippo's house.

'Right,' he says. 'There's a long line of cars parked one behind the other here. Stick a leaflet under the windscreen wiper of the first one, then move on to the next one in a straight line. You do this side of the street, I'll do the other.'

Feeling a bit scared, I feel around with the tip of my foot for the edge of the pavement and reach out a gloved hand to feel for the door of the first car. What if the alarm goes off? Or if I get my fingers trapped under the wipers? No, I can't let that happen. For Dad's sake.

And Ottimo is with us, too. He followed us out. If I'm about to bump into something, he'll jump on my feet to warn me.

After ten or so cars, Filippo comes across to my side of the road.

'Have you finished already?' I ask.

'I've gone as far as the no-parking signs. You keep going, I'll do the letter boxes now.'

We continue together for a bit, Ottimo lying in wait between the cars. It's not too difficult, apart from the cold and worrying that the car owners might just toss the leaflets away without looking at them. I mention this to Filippo.

'What if they do? As long as the right person eventually reads it.'

'I know, but would you do this as a job? Flyering, I mean. I've heard it doesn't pay very well.'

'Who told you that?'

'My cousin. He used to do it.'

'I might try it, although I'd much rather be a moped delivery driver.'

'You mean those people who bring food to your house?'

'Yep.'

'Exciting. But just for a bit or forever?'

'Well, maybe until I found a job I really like. Like an airline pilot.'

'You need to study for that.'

'A writer then.'

I do another couple of cars without replying.

'You know, I can see you as a writer,' I say.

'Thanks. I could see you as one as well.'

'What, as a writer?'

'Yes. Remember the book you started last year?'

'Two years ago.'

'Well, I liked it. Why don't you finish it?'

'Because . . .'

The sound of a flute playing melodiously distracts me from our conversation. 'Who's that?'

'The hippy, musical woman. She's set up a stall in the square outside the church.'

'What is she selling?'

'No idea. Stuff with feathers on . . .'

We go closer. The music gets louder. The musical lady must have a radio on.

'Where are you going?'

'I'm going to give her a leaflet.'

I make my way over to her like I'm sleepwalking. I know the square well. I know there's nothing in the middle of it, no fountain, no trees, no monuments. I just follow the music.

There's a lovely smell rising up from the stall, of leather and incense, but not the kind of incense you get in church. My dream pops back into my head, images of me running across the meadow . . . somehow the smell of the stall makes me feel like a wild animal, running free.

'Can I help you?'

A young-sounding voice, deep but gentle, like Dad's coffee. The musical woman.

'Um, yes. What are these?' I ask, running my fingers over the first things I come to, feeling feathers, coarse little pouches, woven bracelets, bowls.

'Amulets. I made them. Buy two and you get a third one free.'

'How much?'

'Depends. Which one do you want?'

'I, um, I'm not sure. Can I touch them?'

The musical woman doesn't reply but she moves and I feel her by my side. 'I see you're a friend of the spirits of nature. Welcome to my stall.'

'Whaaaat?' Filippo shrieks at my side.

Me, a friend of the spirits of nature? The woman laughs, a light, airy sound, a coffee-coloured butterfly.

'The cat. You don't see them out with humans very often. Of their own accord, I mean. But please tell him I'd rather he didn't sharpen his claws on my blanket. It's the only one I have.'

Ottimo Turcaret! Evidently you've already met this fascinating lady, eh? Ottimo, come here!

My cat swishes a couple of times against my legs, I pet him, then Filippo ends up having to pick him up. He complains how heavy Ottimo is.

'What are your names?'

'I'm Mafalda. He's Filippo.'

'I'm Elsa.'

I was expecting a different kind of name. Maybe Sunset Star or something. Not to worry, Elsa it is.

'And he's Ernesto.'

A whimper from behind the stall. Her dog. 'He's enormous!' Filippo cries.

'He certainly is. And black. Look how black he is! Ernesto, my big, beautiful boy.'

More whimpering. 'Ernesto loves cuddles. And he doesn't growl at cats.'

'Achoo!' Ernesto also has a cold.

'Sorry, he's allergic to pollen. And melon. And white chocolate and horsehair. Here, take this, it's a dreamcatcher.'

Elsa puts a kind of netting made of sticks in my hand; the sticks make a lovely noise as they knock against each other. There are feathers hanging from it. And charms, too, also made of wood. I take off one of my gloves and run my fingertips over the carvings – I feel the moon, a flower . . . and a cat!

'You should hang it up by a window – it will tinkle in the breeze.'

I adore my dreamcatcher. To be honest, it feels magical. It also feels like it should be mine. I rummage discreetly in my pocket to check how much money I have left.

'How much is it?'

'Eight euros.'

I probably have around four. I tell Filippo. I must look

distraught because he offers me his last two euro.

'What will you do tonight?'

I picture him shrugging his shoulders. 'I'll hoover.'

We show Elsa the coins, even though it's not eight euros. 'That's fine,' she says, and places the dreamcatcher in a paper bag.

'Thank you.'

I feel close to tears. I haven't been this happy about a gift since Mum and Dad gave me the blanket Grandma Alba made.

'Wait.'

Elsa takes my wrist and ties something around it. A cord bracelet with an embroidered charm in the middle.

'What colour is it?' I ask Filippo.

'Green,' he replies, 'with a tree on it. Here, in the middle, can you feel it?'

'It will bring you luck, Mafalda.'

I look at the musical woman and am lost for words. How I wish I could see her! Her shadow seems huge in my darkness. Really huge.

'There is something similar to this, Mafalda, called a spirit chaser, but I much prefer dreamcatchers.'

On the subject of chasing, there's a sudden commotion on the other side of the square, coming roughly from the entrance to the church. A loud voice snaps the cold air. 'Are you still here? You've been warned already: no selling in front of the church! If you don't leave now, I'm calling the police!'

'Hey kids, got to run!'

I hear fabric rustling, bowls being dragged and thrown somewhere, probably into a bag. 'Where are you going?'

'I don't know. Somewhere else,' Elsa says.

Filippo pulls my arm. 'Let's go.'

'Do you have anywhere to sleep tonight?' I ask.

'The Mezzani shelter. If it's not full.'

The Mezzani shelter is the only place for people with no home to go to. Without stopping to think about it, I take out a leaflet, a pen, and write my address on it (I hope it's legible) and hand it to Elsa. 'You can come here if you want. There's a shed in the garden. It's a bit dirty, but . . .'

Elsa grabs the leaflet and starts running, not very fast though because she has the stall (it must be a folding table) to carry along with everything else. 'Thank you!' she shouts, her voice receding into the distance. 'Ernesto bello, come here!'

She gives him a short, direct whistle. The next thing we know, Filippo and I are alone, just the two of us standing in the empty square. It's as if she was never there.

'On the first floor,' said Herbert. Which was not at all what I meant, for I had intended my question to apply to his means. 'I have never seen him, for he has always kept his room overhead, since I have known Clara. But I have heard him constantly. He makes tremendous rows — roars, and pegs at the floor with some frightful instrument.'

'Hey! Young lady! You down there!'

I press pause on the player. The whistle touched my ears, even though it wasn't that loud. Who's that calling me?

'Up here, on the balcony!'

I stand up, leave Ottimo in the shadow cast by the garden shed, lolling in his own warm bubble on the cold grass.

'Good day, Mr Rossi.'

'I'll give you good day. I was sleeping.'

'At five in the afternoon?'

'Mind your own business. What are you listening to?'

'A book for school.'

'It's *Great Expectations*, isn't it?'

'Yes. Do you know it?'

A slap on the balcony railings. 'Ah-hah! Do I know it? It's one of my favourites. But don't sit down there listening to it please, it's far too noisy. Put on a pair of those thingamajigs . . .'

'Headphones. Sorry, I'll go and get them.'

I step forward but he calls out to me again. 'No, no, wait. Do me a favour, will you. There's a small watering can in the shed. I think I left it on the right side. I need it for my houseplants. Can you bring it up to me?'

'Yes.'

'OK, I'll wait up here for you.'

The French window bangs shut. He must've gone back inside. Great, now I have to look for his stupid watering can and take it up to him.

I go inside the shed, take small steps down the right-hand side, touching Dad's tools and those of our neighbours. How long is it since Dad last cut the grass? Just as well it's winter. Aha, that's what I'm looking for: a small, watering-can shaped object. I pick it up and am retracing my steps when something special reaches my nose. The smell of leather and incense. I look back into the crisp dark of the shed. Could Elsa have slept in here last night?

Knock.

Mr Rossi takes ages to answer the door.

'Oh, well done young lady.'

He snatches the watering can from my hands with not a word of thanks and shuffles back inside. Slipper noises. Unsure what to do next, I turn around to go back down the stairs. 'Where are you going? Come inside!'

There's a smell of books inside Mr Rossi's apartment, books which haven't seen a duster in years. And the scent of lemon and milky coffee. It's not unpleasant. I advance slowly because I don't know the flat but a hand with sagging skin squeezes my wrist. 'This way. The house has the same layout as yours downstairs. Brave girl. Take a seat here.'

I sink into a very comfortable velvet armchair. I hear Mr Rossi turn on a tap somewhere, then walk at a snail's pace back into the room I'm sitting in and pour water onto the ground. No, not on the ground. He's watering his plants.

'What plants do you have?'

'Lemon. Avocado. Basil. Fig.'

'Avocado?'

'Yes, avocado. Is there something wrong with avocado?'

'No, no, it's just that . . .'

'Can I get you something to drink?'

'No, I . . .'

'Good. Switch that thing on then . . .'

I press play and the narrator resumes Pip's story.

'In looking at me and then laughing heartily, Herbert for the time recovered his usual lively manner. 'Don't you expect to see him?' said I.'

'Oh, how wonderful!' Mr Rossi gushes dreamily.

I press stop.

'One of Dickens' best books.'

'Have you read them all?'

I'm trying to be polite but I'm also a little curious now.

'Dickens and lots more!'

I hear him shuffle across the room and busy himself with something on the far wall. 'Here, this is *The Iliad*. By Homer. And this is Dante's *Inferno*. *Wuthering Heights*, then . . . let's see, here it is, *Great Expectations*!'

He comes over and drops a pile of books on me. They're all big and heavy. I sink even deeper into the armchair. I touch them all, one by one, caressing the covers and fanning the pages in front of my face: aah! That lovely paper smell. How I miss it.

'Do you collect old books?'

'I used to be an actor . . .'

Wow! I've never met an actor before.

'And I'm also a book worm, clearly. I have a proposal to put to you, young lady. Listen up.'

So I have a job.

Mr Rossi and I agreed that I will help him with some errands – like going to the pharmacy, buying bread, watering the plants, dusting off his books – at least twice a week.

'My daughter struggles to visit more than once a month. It's not enough.'

'Don't you have grandchildren who could help you?'

'No. There's just me and these spindly legs.'

That brought a smile to my face, and to Mr Rossi's.

'But Mr Rossi, I might have to get my friend to help me run the errands. I'm not that good out and about on my own.'

'As you wish.'

To be honest, it's quite nice that Mr Rossi says to do things my way. It's like he believes I can actually do all the things he's asking me to do.

In exchange, Mr Rossi will tell me about the books I need to know for school, faster than the speed of light, he says. I have my doubts about that part, but I guess if I don't try . . .

And he says he'll tell me about all the books Filippo needs as well. I won't be earning any money but as first jobs go, I guess it's not too bad.

6

A Deafening Silence
(Bar One Stolen Candle)

'You so fell for it. And now you are having a big birthday party! I love it. And you should do – it's your thirteenth party, it's a big deal!'

Filippo's helping me put balloons up around the flat. Yes, I did fall for it in the end. Stupid Mafalda, stupid, stupid, stupid! Debbie got me into this mess and I didn't even try to get myself out of it, despite smelling trouble from the beginning. I'm talking about my birthday party obviously. A month ago I was scrapping with her in the changing rooms, today I'm standing waiting for my guests to arrive. I can't believe I actually went along with it.

I'm scared of parties! You need to dance in the dark, maybe even kiss someone. But then again, I'm at an advantage because I'm already in the dark. Let's just hope I don't knock the drinks table over.

Mum was super happy to have a party for me despite being so busy all the time. When I tried to get out of it, saying we didn't have the money, she completely brushed it off and sounded more excited than me! 'It's your thirteenth birthday, Mafalda, we have to do something special!' she bubbled, excitedly. She even took me to the shopping centre to get me a new skirt, balloons and a decent cake.

'That skirt really suits you!' Mum said when she popped her head around the changing-room door. I hate it when she does that but I forgave her today because she found two whole hours to spend with me!

I turned down her offer of plaits again today, although I let her run a brush through my hair. We discovered that my hair bounces back into curls even if we comb it right through to the ends. To keep it tidy, we ended up tying it into two low ponytails, just below my ears.

'Do you think the teacher will know I haven't read the whole book?'

Filippo jumps down from a chair and squeaks a balloon in my face. 'Can't say I've given it much thought. It doesn't really matter, though, does it? Your Mr Bossy's going through it point-by-point, he's hardly making it up as he goes along.'

'It's Rossi, not Bossy. Anyway, can you help Mum get the mini-quiches out of the fridge? There's something I need to do.'

. . .

'Dad.'

The silence is deafening. I never thought silence could fill a whole room. 'Dad?'

He's not lying down. Instead, he's sitting on the edge of the bed, by the window. I hear him breathing. Then a long, looooong sigh. 'What is it, Mafalda?'

'My school friends are coming today for my birthday.'

'I know. Mum told me.'

'I don't mind that you didn't say happy birthday. But I wanted to tell you it would mean the world to me if you came through for the cake.'

Another deafening silence. I tiptoe quietly backwards in the direction of the door. I've just about pulled it shut when I smell the salty scent of the sea. Tears. Dad's tears smell of the sea. But if the sea is such a beautiful thing, why does the smell of Dad's tears hurt so much?

My schoolmates are all here, all except two of them who have flu. Debbie was last to arrive. She handed me a gift – a swimming costume that's two sizes too big – and hurried away to dance with her friends.

'Did you like my gift?' Filippo asks, standing at the table with the crisps and popcorn and having to raise his voice over the music to be heard.

'Yes, thanks. Where did you get it?'

'Let's go outside.'

We go onto the balcony. Shutting the door behind us just about blocks out the music.

'I love the belt! It's so soft.'

'It's not a belt, it's a headband. You said you wanted a headband like the one your grandma wore at her wedding.'

'Oh, that's right, so I did!'

'I bought it at the hippy lady's stall.'

'Thank you. Sorry if I didn't realise what it is. I can't even see things with my fingers now either.'

'Oh, Mafalda, stop it.'

It's 9 p.m. and the sun has gone down for the night. Mr Rossi as well, I bet. He'll probably give me a ticking off tomorrow for the noise of the party.

Did I mention that since I've been in the dark, I always know – exactly – what time it is?

'Sometimes it drives me crazy not knowing what's going on. All the things I'd find out if only they could fix my eyes! Maybe that the sky will have turned purple and cherries are blue . . .' I say to Filippo.

He laughs. 'Oh, no need to worry about any of that. Everything is just the same. Seriously, though, if you were to get your sight back, would it scare you?'

'I don't know. Filippo, this is who I am now. I'm in the dark and I can't stand having tidy hair. I like going out cycling with you, playing the guitar without music and recording an audio diary.'

'And?'

'Don't you get it? If I got my sight back, my life would change again, loads.'

'Hey, you could still do all the things you just said even if you were to see again.'

'I know, but . . .'

'But?'

'Maybe I'm scared of seeing again.'

'Well, to be fair, it would be awful if you saw me again for the first time in two years and didn't like my face any more . . .'

'Who said I liked it before?'

We laugh. I turn to him and caress his face, starting from his forehead and running my finger down his nose, across his cheeks, along his chin.

'You're all sweaty. But you feel the same as two years ago.'

'You're the same, too. Well, different, but the same.'

'What do you mean, different but the same?'

Ottimo Turcaret squishes gently through my legs. Someone must've let him out.

'How can I put it, you're different . . . bigger.'

'Taller? Do you know what I would do if I could see again? Count how many steps there are from when I see the cherry tree to when I'm right up next to it, touching its branches.'

'Mafalda. Let's make a deal. Let's be friends forever. Then, if neither of us has found someone to marry by the time we're thirty, the two of us will get hitched.'

I laugh. 'That's ridiculous. But OK, I'm in.'

I put out a hand for him to squeeze. He doesn't.

'What's up?'

'You're not taking it seriously. We need to seal the pact. In fact, let's get married. Right here, right now.'

Is he completely out of his mind? I have no idea what my life will be like, what I'll be like, when I'm grown up. Will I ever get out of the dark? Can Filippo really be sure he wants a wife . . . who's blind? There, I've said it, for the first time ever. It's such a relief to finally admit it, even if it's just in my head.

Anyway, I still have too many unanswered questions. I need time. 'OK, how about we give ourselves three months from today?'

'OK. Where shall we meet?'

My attention happens to fall on the empty darkness at the bottom of the garden. At the same time, I feel Filippo touch the bracelet the musical woman gave me, the one with the tree charm on it.

'Beneath the cherry tree.'

'What time?'

'Do you remember when you used to send me light signals when we were up in the mountains? At midnight. It was beautiful.'

'How are we going to meet in the middle of the night? Let's make it midday. It's easier.'

'OK, agreed. So we'll meet in three months' time. That's the first of May, midday, outside school.'

'And we'll get married.'

'OK. Providing we don't marry anyone else before that!' I laugh.

He doesn't laugh.

'Filippo, are you coming inside for a dance?' Heat and the smell of pizza from inside. A droning voice and the sickly sweet smell of jelly beans. It's Debbie.

'We're coming.'

I go back inside and dance too, with Roly, with my schoolfriends, even with a bottle of Fanta. I dance to take my mind off Filippo dancing with Debbie. There's a smell of petrol in the air and I realise it's coming from me, from my heart.

Mum comes in singing 'Happy Birthday'.

'Mum, I told you to stay through there!'

But everyone is singing and she doesn't hear me. I find myself pushed to the middle of the room, the heat of the candle flames warming my face. When the song ends, I blow them all out. Or nearly all – there's always one that won't go out.

I feel its warmth fade though.

Someone else must've blown it out.

'Happy birthday, Mafalda!'

'Dad!'

I jump on him, squeeze him tight. He did it, he got up and came to see me! The best birthday present ever. Even though he stole my candle.

I'm in the tree.

'Mafalda, throw us down some cherries!'

Who's down there?

Girls, you're back! It's so nice to see you all. Estella, Grandma . . . Elsa, you too! Daniela, who brought you? Your dad? I didn't think boys knew about this meadow. Just my squishy cat. You look so pretty dressed in those clothes! Are you having a party? Thank goodness I kept my red skirt on.

There you are. Have some cherries. Grandma, move, or they'll land on your head!

Hang on a sec, I'll move over to that branch there – it has more cherries. Girls, you wouldn't believe what I can see from up here – so many red clouds blowing in . . .

Oh no! I missed my footing! I'm falling, girls, help! I can't see you any more! Where have you gone? Why has it gone all dark? Why can't I see any more, not even in my dreams? Why?

I'm falling . . .'

'Mum!'

The darkness is everywhere – in my room, in the flat in the world. It's 3.30 a.m., I'm sure of it. The silence is only ever this big at this time of night. It's scary. I can't move.

'Mum!'

'Mafalda, what is it?'

'Dad. What are you doing up?'

Sitting up in bed between damp sheets (nightmares don't half make you sweat!) I look towards the dark, dark door and Dad's dark shadow.

'I heard you cry out in your sleep and I ran through. Were you having a bad dream?'

'Yes. Can you stay with me until I fall back asleep?'

He comes over and sits on the edge of the bed. We rock together. He tucks me in. 'Snuggle back under, it's cold. Let me cover you up a little more. Ah, Mafalda . . .'

'What?'

Click. The light on my bedside lamp. 'I think you're going to need your mum this time. Wait here, I'll go and get her.'

'Mum . . .'

There she is, mint ice lolly and violet.

'Mum, my head aches. Maybe I drank too much Coke at the party.'

'It's not the Coke, darling. Put your slippers on, I'll take you into the bathroom.'

'Why?'

She sits on the edge of the bed as well, strokes my hair against the pillow, like she used to do when I was little. 'Do you remember when we saw the doctor last year?'

'When I had German measles?'

'No, sweet pea. That time we went to her big office, with all the girls in your class. She talked about periods, remember?'

Heck. Oh heck.

'You've started your period, Mafalda. But there's nothing to worry about. It's not a bad thing. Let's go through to the bathroom and –'

'I don't want it, Mum!'

I'm close to tears. I only remember bits of what the doctor said, one most of all: blood. I'm scared.

Mum gives a soft laugh. 'Sweet pea, no one wants it. But it is what it is. It means everything's working properly. You'll get used to it.'

I venture out from under the covers, rest my head on Mum's shoulder. 'How long will it last? I remember twenty-eight days. I don't want to lose blood for that long. I won't have any left.'

'No, no, Mafalda! The bleeding only lasts three or four days. The rest of the month, your body will produce eggs and then slowly expel them.'

'Are the eggs something to do with becoming a mum?'

Mum takes my face between her hands. 'That's exactly why you need the eggs. For that, and as an excuse to eat a whole lot of ice cream every month. We'll do that together every single month from now on, Mafalda, I promise. And guess what? Women in the same family tend to get their periods at the same time of the month. They synchronise with each other.'

'Really? Have you got yours?'

'I'm due to start the day after tomorrow.'

'Ah, how do you know?'

Mum smiles into the night-time darkness, which is suddenly filled with words, beautiful words like ice cream, mum, synchronise. 'Come on, let's go into the bathroom then we'll head to the kitchen. There's a lot I have to explain.'

'Mum . . . how would I manage without you? Who would explain all this to me?'

'Dad. He knows all about periods! Remember, he lives with us two girls and has a sister and lots of friends who are girls.'

'Mum . . .'

'What, sweet pea?'

'Now that I've got my period, do I have to become a mum?'

'My love, being parents to someone has nothing to do with the bleeding.'

'But I thought . . .'

'One day you'll understand. Come on, let's go look for a pad. And a bowl of ice cream. I bagsy the chocolate chip though.'

'OK, it's yours.'

Monday morning, desire to go to school zero. Filippo sent me an audio message at 07.15: *I've got a temperature, don't wait for me. Speak later.*

Oh no. Thank goodness Ottimo takes me. Or maybe I should say that I take him. He's a laid-back cat, no tests to take, no weird friends with a temperature to contend with. Ottimo is not the kind of cat to chase butterflies either. He'd be much more likely to look down his nose at a butterfly or have it ride on his back.

I went to Mr Rossi's yesterday, even though I was tired after the party and . . . everything else.

He says he didn't hear a thing the night of my party, then changed his story to say that he didn't hear a thing EXCEPT for the tremendous ear-busting commotion that went on all night. He does like to exaggerate! My friends left at eleven o'clock – Debbie was the last one to go – so it was all quiet long before midnight!

'We had such a brilliant time when I was an actor. The show would finish at midnight and we'd paint the town red all night with the rest of the cast!'

'What town?' I ask to be polite but also to get out of the dusting. It's not easy to dust in the dark and I never know if I'm doing it right. It's more interesting listening to his stories. Old people are all the same. They complain but then you find out they were up to the same thing, or worse, when they were young.

'Rome, Naples, Syracuse, ah, Syracuse! Then La Scala theatre in Milan . . . Did I ever tell you about the time we flew to Japan for *Madam Butterfly*? That's where I met my wife.'

'Was your wife Japanese?'

'No, she was from Verona. What's Japanese got to do with it?'

Oops, I think I've lost him. He gets confused sometimes. I like his stories though.

Yesterday he told me the story of Pip's life in minute detail. He wanted to start the next book as well but Mum called me back for dinner.

'Great party.'

Eugh. Debbie and her jelly-bean breath this early on a Monday morning.

'Today's switch seats day,' I remind her.

For once she doesn't reply.

Tuesday, Filippo is still unwell. I go into town with Mum to look for a new pencil case. Mine broke and she wasn't able to fix the zip.

Mum also pops into the dry-cleaner. She always does that – she sees a place then remembers that she has to go in. Wait here, she tells me, and goes inside.

I wander away a little. I don't like the smell of the ironing spray. I kick a stone, follow it, then kick it again along the pavement. I brush against something with my side, a small table . . . the musical woman's stall! I hear her milky coffee voice.

'Hiya. It's Mafalda, isn't it?'

'Yes.'

A wet nose touches my hand. Ernesto. I pat his head. He sneezes, all over my shoes no doubt. The smell of Ottimo's fur on me must've set him off.

'So, did you hang up your dreamcatcher?'

Oh no. I forgot. To be honest, I can't do it myself and was hoping Dad would help me. He's good at that sort of thing, hammering and nails and all that. But . . .

'I haven't decided where to put it,' I lie.

'No problem. Are you looking for something else?'

'No, no . . . I was wondering, did you happen to sleep in our shed?'

'Yes, a couple of nights ago. It was too cold on the street.'

'Have you ever had a home, Elsa?'

I know it's rude to ask personal questions, but I'm curious.

'I certainly did! My parents are still alive, you know. They work in a bank.'

'So you're not poor then!'

Elsa squeezes my nose with two fingers and I hear a smile in her voice. 'I am, but not the way you think. I choose to live like this.'

'But . . . why?'

She cackles. 'Just because. One day I'll tell you a story about a girl who was a bit rebellious, a boyfriend who was tired of being a boyfriend and a deep loathing for banks.'

Ernesto sneezes again.

'What's up baby? Are you cold? I think we'll be booking into the shed hotel again tonight,' she says, and I almost feel like I can see her – tall, shivering and winking in my direction.

'Let's go, Mafalda!'

I run to Mum's car. I remember roughly where she parked it. I'm about to get in when Mum exclaims, 'Isn't that Filippo?'

Who? Where?

'There's a boy that looks like him at the other end of the street,' Mum says. 'Big, baggy purple jacket, ladies' bike. I swear it's him. I'd recognise him in a crowd anywhere. If he looks this way, I'll wave.'

'Mum, call him over! He must be better!'

'No, no,' she says, lowering her voice. 'Let's not. He's with a girl.'

We get into the car.

I sit through the trip home like I'm perched on a flying carpet which, instead of taking me on an adventure, flies me through a dark tunnel full of questions. Who was the girl? Was it Debbie? Why did Filippo say he wasn't well? If it was just a friend, he would've rung me to go out with them. So what is she, then, if she's not a friend? And what do I care? Has he found a new best friend? But why? Why? Why? Why?

At dinner, when Mum turned around to get a spoon out the drawer, I hid my toasted sandwich under my jumper. Mum got suspicious right away. 'You finished that quickly. Try not to eat so fast, Mafalda! You'll choke.'

It made me want to giggle, because the same thing happens to Pip in front of his sister's husband, only with bread and jam. Pip's the main character in the first book the teacher gave us to read at school, and he needs to take food to Magwitch, who has just run away from prison – a *fugitive*.

'Do you want me to take the rubbish out?'

'Aren't you being helpful? Working for Mr Rossi is obviously doing you good, or is there something I should know?'

I get up from the table before she gets any more suspicious. It's not easy hiding something from your mum. I sneak outside, leave the rubbish in the alleyway, and cross the garden. It's night-time. I trip over a tree root. Who remembered that was there?

'Elsa?'

The shed is still empty. I go further inside, unzip my jacket and pull out a packet of biscuits and the toasted sandwich from my dinner. I leave them for her. I hope she finds them.

Click.

Mafalda here, from under the covers.
    It's the eighteenth of February, the school holidays seem light years away, and any

83

motivation to get up in the morning, well, let's just say that's hiding under the covers as well.

Memo for this afternoon: take a warm blanket out to the garden shed for Elsa, maybe the one Grandma made. The food I took out was all gone the next day, so she must have decided to stay the night.

The cherry tree seems to be hibernating these days as well. I've never felt it so far away, not even when I had to take hundreds of steps just to smell its scent.

7

A Horrible Age

'What's up young lady? Something on your mind?'

'Nothing, Mr Bossy Rossi.'

He hates it when I call him that, but it's just a bit of fun.

'Less of the Bossy. You can call me Nino.'

He sits down in his armchair, which gives only the faintest puff under his frail and ancient frame. I water the avocado and try not to splash damp earth onto the floor.

'You seem worried.'

'No, just feeling a bit weird.'

'That's normal. How old are you? Twelve?'

'Thirteen.'

'Oh, that's a terrible age. Though I'm eighty-six and still get that weirdness. But I've grown accustomed to feeling different by now.'

'How did you manage that, Nino?' I remember to use his first name quite easily, maybe because we're talking about something so personal, what it feels like to be different.

'I decided to grit my teeth. They were my own back then. Got to grit my dentures now.'

I giggle into the plants so he won't hear me.

'All my friends from primary school, and almost all of them from secondary, put down roots, had families, found permanent jobs. Not me. I wanted to study, to act, to travel! Which was a massive disappointment for my father, who had high hopes I would take over the family business, have a glittering career and give him litters of grandchildren.'

'What happened in the end?'

'Well, I did eventually give him a granddaughter but I still never saw him again.'

'Wasn't that really upsetting?'

Mr Rossi gets up from the armchair with a huff and takes the watering can out of my hands. 'You're flooding the place. Here, this is how you do it. Not seeing my father again was a liberation.'

Silence. The rustle of leaves between us.

'And also the most excruciating pain I've ever felt in my whole life. Bring me *Jonathan Livingston Seagull*, will you? We can make a start on that.'

Click.

Memo: be like everyone else, or be truly special.

End of February.

The sun came out for a few days, then it started raining. I love the rain because it frees all the smells that were locked away until just a few seconds before! I used to play a seasonal smells game with Dad. Many of the flowers that blossom in gardens around town remind him of when he was young. I loved listening to his stories.

Dad was almost normal for a while after my birthday party. He even went to an interview but they ended up giving the job to someone else. We don't know why. He's been back in his bedroom since then, in the dark, doing nothing.

The disappointment is worse than the worry if you ask me. It's like when you queue to get onto a ride, you stand there for two hours because everyone's told you it's amazing, then when it's finally your turn, you discover it lasts less than a minute and you're back at the start before you know it, thinking, is this it?

I had such high hopes for that interview.

The rain is amazing, but it brings the cold back with it. And I keep thinking about Elsa and Ernesto.

I pick up Grandma's patchwork blanket and go outside. Water is still running off the canopy roof but I'm going to try. 'Come with me, Ottimo!'

I walk through the mud in the garden and Ottimo Turcaret nearly trips me up trying to keep himself dry. What a selfish cat he can be!

The shed is damp and there's a rake missing. I notice straight away because it's usually propped against the door to keep it tight shut. It doesn't matter. I just want to leave the blanket for Elsa. I move deeper into the shed.

In the spot where I left the toasted sandwich and biscuits the other day, I find something. Or my cat finds it and starts playing with it. What is it? A ball of paper? 'Give it here, silly squishy.'

It's a piece of paper folded in four.

How exciting! Has Elsa written me a letter? I have to get someone to read it to me right away. I go back inside and straight up to Mr Rossi's flat.

'I was sleeping.'

'Hey Nino, you're always sleeping. Come on, get your glasses, I want to know what this paper says!'

I sit down on the rug by Nino's chair.

'Let's see. *Dear Mafalda* . . .'

Yes! It's a letter. I knew it!

'Thank you for the food you left me. Ernesto loved the toasted sandwich. I hope you don't mind but I gave him the ham because I don't eat meat. The rest was delicious.

'I was thinking about our last chat. There'll be things you might be wondering. I wanted to say that everything depends on your point of view. You might think I'm mad, many people do – I had

88

a family and a job once and I chucked it all away.

'The fact is that life is full of surprises, some good, some bad. Some so bad they knock you for six. Some people are strong and manage to say, "It's OK, it doesn't matter," while others break down. If the boyfriend I had at the time hadn't left me, for example, maybe now I wouldn't be the "weird hippy woman" selling bracelets on the street. I was so in love with him, you know. We were going to be married.

'But maybe it wasn't all his fault. Maybe I was always going to become the weird hippy woman at some point. Something in me went a bit haywire. Now it's just me, looking out for myself, and kind people like you who give me a helping hand every now and then. But never forget, Mafalda, the only person who can look after you, now and forever, is you.

'One more thing, Mafalda. You can't wait for other people to change their opinion of you. To be happy, you have to change the way you think about yourself. It's not easy to explain. Maybe we'll chat about it again one day. E.'

I sigh. What an amazing letter. I need to think about all the things in it, but I'm so happy she wrote, even though I feel bad for Elsa and her broken engagement. Gosh, could she be a kind of Miss Havisham? I picture her shut away in a room, wedding dress on, wedding cake with cobwebs all over it, feeling desperately sad. No! Elsa is much better off as she is now, living outdoors, free. A bit sad, maybe, but free.

'Who the heck is this E?' Nino exclaims.

'A musician friend of mine.'

'My word! How interesting. Can you introduce me?'

I laugh. 'Mr Rossi, Elsa must be at least fifty years younger than you!'

'So what?' he barks. 'Love comes in many different forms, you know, more ways than you think.'

Filippo's face suddenly pops up in front of me, and I feel sad. I haven't spoken to him in ages. I did a bit of digging at school but no one could tell me if he's going out with Debbie. There is someone else I could ask, but I don't think I have the courage.

'So, my lady, shall we get a move on? Can you pick up my heart pills from the chemist, please? Wait, I'll get you the prescription and the money. We'll finish *Jonathan Livingston Seagull* when you come back.'

The hardest thing in the world is to convince a bird that he is free!

I make up my mind on the way to the pharmacy. I need to know for sure about Filippo, so I have to go and find the one person who might be able to tell me.

I pay for Grandpa Nino's prescription (Grandpa? OK, Grandpa it is, I guess) then take the road out to the villa

I want to go to. I'm positive I can remember it, even in the dark, because I must've walked it hundreds of times when I was young and could see.

Chiara and I haven't spoken much since going to big school. Just 'Hiya' and little more. But I know she goes to athletics with Debbie, Daniela and some other girls in my class, and sometimes they go to the pizza parlour together. Debbie hangs out with Chiara at break. She has to know something about Debbie and Filippo.

It's all so complicated. The last time I went to her house I could still see. I never imagined we'd stop being friends one day. But then again, I never imagined I'd lose my sight either. Life really is a box of surprises. Nasty ones, sometimes. Every time I open the box, though, I keep hoping I'll get a nice one. Sooner or later.

My hand skims some railings and I'm about to try to cross the road, summoning all my courage, when I hear car doors bang just ahead of me.

'Mafalda, what are you doing here?'

'Hi, Chiara.'

'Hi, Mafalda! How nice to see you dear! Do you want to come in for tea? Does your mum know you're here by yourself?' Chiara's mum gives me the third degree.

'Yes, she knows. I can't stop, though. Thanks all the same.'

'OK. I'll go inside and put the groceries away.'

'I'll be in in a minute,' Chiara tells her.

Chiara comes over to me. She's always known when I need to talk to her. Even now. 'What's up?'

'I need to ask you something.'

'Fire away.'

I take a deep breath. 'Is it true that Debbie's going out with Filippo?'

'What, don't you know? Aren't you two supposed to be best friends?'

My cheeks burn red hot. I don't know what to say.

Chiara sighs. I wonder if her hair is still straight, low ponytail, fringe.

'OK, I'll tell you, but it's a mega secret. If Debbie finds out I told you she'll kill me. They're not really an item. They meet up. They've been out twice. That's all.'

'Don't worry. I won't say anything. What else do you know?'

'Well, I shouldn't even have told you that – you have to promise not to tell anyone.'

'I promise.'

'Debbie told me that Filippo only went out with her because he thinks you don't like him, and –'

'He thinks I don't like him?'

'Yes, and she took advantage of that. She's telling all her friends that they're going out, but I know she only likes him because he's older. And . . . Mafalda . . .'

'What?'

'Is it true they're going to cure your eyes?'

'Did Debbie tell you that?'

'Yes, and she told Filippo, too. He was really upset you didn't tell him yourself.'

'Chiara, Maria's on the phone for you!'

'I'm coming! I have to go now. I'll see you at school.'

I turn and walk away, giving Chiara a wave.

What a mess. That's why Filippo doesn't want to see me. He thinks I hid the fact that my eyes are going to be cured. It's not even true!

He likes me. I should've been less hesitant when he asked me to marry him. I should have said yes straight away. Debbie has messed it all up. It's too late now.

I run, slowly at first, then faster. Mafalda, you're such an idiot!

'Dad, are you awake?'

I go into my parents' bedroom, tiptoeing, scared of disturbing him.

Dad's awake, shifts a little and asks me what's wrong. I think he was gazing out the window, even though the shutters are always shut. I throw myself onto the bed beside him.

'Dad . . .'

'What's up?'

I can't think of anything special to tell him, nothing that would cheer him up. I'd like to talk to him about Filippo. He's a man and, in theory, thinks like a man, so maybe he could give me some man-related advice. I stroke the sheets and my fingertips touch a box that Dad has on his lap. 'What's that?'

'My records.'

'The boogie-woogie ones? Shall we dance? Go on, teach me!'

I jump off the bed. I'd do anything to get him out of bed. He's looking at me, I swear.

'Dancing in the dark is like dancing in the light. You don't need me to teach you.'

'Come on, Dad! Get up. Let's at least listen to a record!'

'Mafalda, this whole thing . . .'

His voice turns suddenly serious and jittery. I say nothing, just stand there.

'You think I'm good at lots of things . . .'

'You are! You're a great cook, you make amazing pancakes.'

'I just got lucky a couple of times.'

'You repair bikes. I don't know anyone else who can do that.'

'It's all just luck. The right tool at the right time. Mafalda, I –'

'And that photo of the race, what about that?'

'What race?'

'The sprint you did in high school. There's a photo in the hall. You came first that time. That wasn't luck. I saw the medal you won, too, a few years ago.'

'That was just chance. The faster guy was off sick that day. Mafalda, if I was fired, it must've been because of me, there's no other explanation. Clearly they could do without me. They don't get rid of you if you're essential. I was obviously lacking in something . . .'

I go back to him and pummel my fists into his chest. 'Don't say that! Don't!'

'Mafalda, I'm sorry.'

I can't bear it. It's like an iceberg shearing from my heart. I keep beating Dad's chest and he doesn't hug me. He doesn't even try, so I run out of the room, bumping into everything on the way, and shut myself in my bedroom, crying, crumpled on the bed like girls do in films. Only this is real life. Not even Ottimo scratching at my door can save me this time.

With my face pressed into my pillow, I feel around for my recorder. Click.

Cherry Tree, I'm telling you now, I am never setting foot in Dad's room again, not for a month at least. You talk to him. Blow some brown and yellow leaves onto his pillow – he loves them. Wake Grandma up out of her hibernation in your trunk and tell her that her son needs help. You both need to speak to him. I can't bear to see him like this. A tiny part of me died inside today, hearing him talk like that, apologising, saying sorry, Mafalda. Speak to him, please. All I want to do now is sleep and dream of finding the best ever job, one where they can never fire you, not even if you're blind and so useless you need a pretend grandpa to be happy . . .

. . .

Ah-choo!

It's a really loud sneeze, but not as loud as Ernesto the dog's usually are. I'd been hoping to find them here, in the square by the church where we met the first time. I go over to the stall.

'Hi Mafalda! How are you?'

'Hi Elsa! I'm well. And you? Have you got a cold?'

'Nah. Your hearing is a bit too good. It was just dust in my nose. Do you want to buy something?'

'Yes, I got extra pocket money from my mum.'

'What for?'

'Doing well in my test. Can I have another bracelet like mine?'

Elsa roots around her table then hands me a small parcel and takes my five euros.

'Aaahhhhh-choo!'

'Wait a sec, Elsa. Here, have a hankie.'

As I hand over a packet of hankies, something falls out of my pocket and lands on the table between me and her.

'What's this?'

Rustle, rustle . . . a sheet of paper opening. My dreams memo! I wrote my dreams for the future down then totally forgot it. I must've given it to Elsa along with the hankies.

'Dream one, be friends with Filippo forever. Two, fly to faraway places. Three . . .'

I reach out and grab for the paper where I think

Elsa's hands are, before she can read any more. 'Stop! It's embarrassing hearing my dreams read aloud.'

'Why? A person's dreams should always be said aloud. Can I give you some advice?'

'Well, if it's nice advice, yes . . .'

'You should tidy up the list. Write it out neater for starters. It's not very clear, sweetie . . .'

'Elsa, I can't see!'

'So what? Practise. We all have to look out for ourselves, remember? And you need to sort out your priorities. Friends are like trees, you know. You need to water them, otherwise they'll die.'

'It's hardly the same thing!'

'Oh, it is. You chose the cherry tree just like you chose Filippo, and now you need each other. One more thing. It takes at least ten dreams for one to come true. Bear that in mind for the future.'

On the way back home I think about what Elsa said. A thought suddenly strikes me like a ray of sun piercing a gemstone – *you chose the cherry tree* . . .

How does Elsa know about my tree?

8

Thank Goodness for People Like Him

Click.

> *Fifth of March. Today's the day of the longest running race of the year.*
>
> *I'm worried about Elsa. I think she's got a fever. She needs her temperature taken but I don't know how I can because our thermometer is broken – I dropped it – and we haven't bought a new one yet.*

'Download the app,' Filippo would say, or more likely he'd go ahead and download it for me. I'm useless. Without him I feel even more in the dark than ever.

It's early in the morning and the whole school is getting

ready for the run.

The emotions of so many people brush the skin on my face, touch my wrists, get into the space between my windproof jacket and my gloves. My cheeks are cold but it doesn't bother me because the heat of everyone else's breath is much stronger in the dark. The hot breath of so many people all together smells like milky coffee and toothpaste.

We're warming up, the girls in my year are starting in ten minutes, the boys after that.

'Remember the first part of the course is the hardest. It'll take almost ten minutes to get round, then there's the path up the hill at the halfway mark. Tell me if it gets too much for you.'

Carola is pacing back and forth between me and the starting line. She's analysing the course.

'Then, we'll pick up the pace as much as we can towards the end, say the last fifty-sixty metres. How does that sound?'

I lift my face towards her. It's obvious she doesn't want to do it. Neither do I, to be honest. 'Miss, can I tell you something in private?'

She leans in. I whisper that I've got my period and would rather not run.

'Are you sure?'

'I'm sure. Shall we go and get a hot chocolate at the runners' refreshments tent?'

. . .

The first group has started.

The pounding of the girls' feet on the cold ground as they run across the field and behind the school grows weaker and weaker. They're getting further away. It'll be a while before they come back this way. The cheering at the starting line peters out as people go back to chatting and stretching.

I blow on the sugary steam rising from my hot chocolate and think of Filippo; he's about to set off with the boys in the year above. Maybe I still have time to wish him good luck, before his race starts.

A tap on my shoulder stops me.

'Are you Mafalda?'

I don't recognise the voice. What I mean is, I know who it is but I don't know *him* at all. I think he's called Luigi and he's the guy who does the school newspaper, *Panino*. Luigi chooses what to write, interviews people, sets out the pages on his computer. He's really talented. He's in class D1. Our English teacher introduced him to us so that we know who to speak to if we want to write an article or place an ad.

'Yes, I'm Mafalda.'

'Listen, I'm running in a bit. I noticed you didn't start with your group . . .'

'No.'

'Lucky for me. I need someone to take the names of the first three in each race and collect some hot comments for *Panino*.'

'Hot comments?'

'What I mean is, catch them as they cross the finish line – stuff like, "I'm exhausted" or "I'm really pleased", the kind of thing you hear on TV.'

Cool. Like a sports reporter. But how do I get the right runner?

'If you're thinking what I think you're thinking, don't worry. I'll help you.'

'Thank you, Carola!' Carola really is kind to me.

'OK, Luigi. If you want, I can record a kind of commentary.'

I show him my voice recorder, always with me in my pocket.

'Fab! We'll put it up on the school website after. Here, Miss, maybe you can get a couple of good photos?'

I imagine he's giving his photo-reporter camera to Carola. Or maybe his mobile phone.

'Good. I better go and get ready to run. Thanks!!'

'Luigi!'

'What?'

'Do you have anything you'd like to say before the race?'

'Fantastic! That's the spirit!'

Home!

Mum stopped by her sister's today to pick up a meat loaf with an apricot in the middle. Delicious!

'So, I rang the dentist and she says you don't need braces on your teeth this year . . .'

Finally, some good news.

'Mr Rossi needs your help today as well. He mentioned a letter to write, but I'm not sure I understood. How did the races go today?'

'Oh, the usual people won – Pietro, Jessica . . .'

'From 9B?'

'Yep.'

'What about Filippo? How did he get on?'

I feel a smile coming on. 'I'm writing a separate article about him for the school newspaper. *Pupil refuses to take part in annual cross-country race event in protest.*'

'In protest about what?' Mum laughs.

'The school system, teachers forcing us all to do the same things, behave in the same way, run on a predefined course . . . that's what he said. Or yelled, rather. You could hear him across the other side of the field.'

'But it was a race. The course has to be predefined!'

'Tell him that. Carola told me all about it in a live report. She said not only did he refuse to start but he also convinced another two or three people in his class not to start with him, the lazier ones, obviously. Mr Muli and the principal had to literally carry him off the course while the other teachers were threatening to fail his classmates in PE if they didn't run. Filippo was shouting that they should ignore it and not take part.'

'A proper insurrectionary.'

I don't know what an insurrectionary is, but if it's someone who's always disrupting things and causing bother about something only he cares about, then yes, Filippo is very much an *insurrectionary*.

'Thank goodness there are people like him in the world, Mafalda. Thank goodness.'

Now I know.

I love Filippo.

I need to find a way to win him back.

Ding-dong. Ding-dong!

Come on, Mr Bossy Rossi, open up!

How slow are you in those slippers?

'Grandpa Nino!'

The sound of keys turning, locks sliding, door opening. 'What did you call me?'

'Grandpa Nino. I need the advice of a man.'

I go inside and flop down on the velvet armchair. By now I know the exact position of every piece of furniture in his flat.

Mr Rossi follows slowly behind me, dragging a chair over to sit beside me. I can almost hear his bones creak, the way squeaky doors creak in horror films. 'I was sleeping,' he says. Mr Rossi sounds grumpy but I know he isn't really. And I have something important to ask him.

'Grandpa Nino, how do I win back someone I really like?'

'Hmm, that's a difficult one. How should I know? I'm too old for these things.'

'Weren't you the one who said love knows no age? Oh, come on, you have to help me!'

'Ask your mother.'

'She's too busy. And I'm too embarrassed.'

'Then ask your father.'

'He's, uh . . . well, I'm too embarrassed to ask him as well.'

'So it's only with me you've no shame? I don't have time either, you know.'

'That's not true! What do you have to do?'

'Boil my dentures.'

'Do it later. I'll help you.'

Mr Rossi gives a hearty laugh. 'You really are desperate if you're willing to boil my dentures for me!'

I wait for him to stop teasing me then I tell him everything. When I'm done, he sits and thinks for a few minutes, then offers the best piece of advice I could ever have expected from him. 'In the classics, when a love story gets a bit bumpy, which is always the case, one of the two makes a grand gesture to win back the other one.'

'A grand gesture? Like something super romantic?'

'Of course. But it must be theatrical and very, very important to the other person. I'm warning you though, there's no guarantee it will work.'

I sit up straight and start to think. 'Grandpa Nino, I

have to try. If I don't try, I'll never know.'

'In the classics, it's always men who do these things.'

'What about the women?'

'They faint, or something similarly bad.'

'Well, I won't faint. No siree. At the moment, I can't think of anything showstopping to do for Filippo. But I'll work on it.'

Maybe a good book would give me inspiration.

'Can you read me a few pages of this one?'

Mr Rossi's favourite book is lying on the side table beside the armchair. I know it's his favourite because he always keeps it there. It's a thick tome with an engraved leather cover. I'm curious.

'This one? It's ideal for your problem. I could recite it word for word if you want. *Happy families are all alike . . .*'

'What's it called?'

'*Anna Karenina*. One day you'll also be bewitched by the beauty of this story.'

'Will you tell me it?'

'We'll work our way through the list of books for school first. I'm not immortal, you know. We mustn't leave any unfinished business, before . . .'

The blood freezes in my veins.

'You're not dying are you, Nino?'

'Of course not, but you never know.'

I imagine him walking towards a bright light, waving to me, and my eyes fill with tears. I banish the thought; Nino would never look so angelic, not even on the other side. He'd probably complain about being woken in the middle of a nap, or demand to go home to take his blood pressure pill, which he left on the bathroom shelf.

He wouldn't be allowed though. You don't get to come back from the other side. I know that. I know lots of people who live there. I must tell Grandpa Nino to visit the cherry tree when the time comes, to say hello to Grandma and Estella in the tree trunk.

Enough. No more sad thoughts.

'So Nino, how about you read to me today?'

'Definitely not, not today, not tomorrow, not ever. I don't like reading aloud.'

'What? I thought you were an actor!?'

'I learned the parts by heart, I didn't just read them out, you know.'

That makes me smile. 'I have a friend who does that, too – Filippo.'

'So he also hates reading aloud?'

'Yes, with a passion. He tries to do it occasionally when he's with me. Maybe it's because he's a slow reader and often stumbles over the letters.'

'Really? What do you mean? Does he mix them up?'

'Sometimes.'

'I bet he always has an excuse not to do any work. He's bright but hates school.'

'Yes! That's it exactly. But how do you know? Do you know him?'

Mr Rossi slaps his hand on his skinny knee. He does

that a lot. 'No, Mafalda, I don't know him. But I think I know why your Filippo behaves like he does.'

'Really?'

'Yes, really. I'd have to hear him read aloud at least once, but I'm pretty certain your friend is dyslexic.'

'What's dyslexic, Nino?'

'It means it's much harder for him to recognise the letters of the alphabet, and therefore also whole words.'

'Is it a serious disease?'

'It's not a disease. It's just the way he is. Short-sighted people need glasses, dyslexics need special practice to learn to read, and more time to do tests.'

Nino is super happy to have worked out Filippo's problem. And I am, too. When you understand what's wrong, the next step is usually to find a way to fix it; this happens for *thousands* of things in life. Everything except my eyes.

No matter. This could be my grand gesture for Filippo!

'Nino, what do you think I can do to help him?'

'You have to tell his mum, or his English teacher. If they don't already know.'

'Do you think they might have realised already? So why haven't they done anything, like take him to a doctor or teach him those exercises?'

'Sometimes we don't join the dots. Until not so long ago, people with dyslexia were just seen as a bit slow, not cut out for school, or even lazy.'

'How do you know all this?'

Nino smiles with his voice – it's a bit of a crooked smile with a tinge of sadness to it. 'Oh, that's easy. I'm dyslexic too.'

'So, Mafalda, you're convinced Filippo is dyslexic?'

The English teacher who takes the older classes taps her pencil on the edge of her desk. It's just the two of us in the room. I waited until break to speak to her.

'Miss, you must have noticed, too.'

'You're right, Mafalda, I'd noticed, but there are no official notes in the register and his parents have never been to parents' night.'

'His parents are complicated. But *you* could add the note! I'm not sure what that means exactly but if it helps him get easier tests . . .'

'You really are a nice girl, Mafalda. But a note is not enough. Filippo's parents will also have to take him to a specialist to diagnose the dyslexia and send me a certificate. Only then will I be allowed, legally, to give him adapted tests and homework.'

'Oh, Miss, there's so much to do. That will take months and he'll fail the year!'

'Not necessarily. He just has to get sixty per cent in each subject. I'll try to put in a good word at the teachers' meeting in June. We'll see what happens . . .'

That's no good. I can't accept a 'we'll see what happens'. Not any more. I need to know now what we can do for Filippo. To know that there's a solution to his problem, unlike mine. That's why I have a secret plan I'm going to suggest to the teacher.

'I actually have another idea. What would you say if . . .'

9

Contours of the Soul

I'm so, so scared to go home from school today.

I dawdle along the pavement, hands gripping the straps of my backpack. I'm scared I've done something way too big and that Filippo will be annoyed with me. It's never easy to tell someone they have a problem. But it will make everything so much easier for him afterwards. If he gets angry that everyone knows he's dyslexic, well, what can I do?

Am I seriously willing to lose Filippo in order to help him? It's too late now anyway. I should've thought about this first. Crikey. I'm so scared I'll bump into him on the way home.

His teacher was going to let him use a calculator for the first time ever in a test today. If anyone in the class said it wasn't fair, she was going to explain very simply that Filippo has different needs from them, and if anyone insisted, she'd make them do the test with the sheet upside down.

'It's practically the same thing for Filippo, doing things without the necessary adaptations,' the teacher explained. 'Of course his classmates will have to be kind and try to keep the secret as best they can. I think they will. But I don't know if Filippo will accept that he's different from them.'

A bicycle bell, behind me. I turn around. Is it him?

The bike races past without slowing.

Ottimo Turcaret slinks up with a quiet miaow. I pick him up and carry him home.

Elsa's tall shadow is just ahead of me. I found her in the garden shed this time: she and Ernesto were settling in for the night when I went down to give her an aspirin. I got it from the bathroom cabinet; I locked myself in, even though Mum has banned me from doing that, and rummaged through the medicine box. I hope I picked out the right packet. From the smell you can't tell what kind of medicine it is. I shoved a couple of boxes in my pocket. They felt the right size, the way I remembered them.

Elsa has a bad cough, today, Ernesto too. From outside, I hear her trying to hold it in, but she can't, and when she takes the medicine I've brought, the hand that brushes my fingers is burning hot. 'I think what you did for your friend was amazing, Mafalda. With your friend's teacher,

I mean. Shake my hand.'

'Why?'

'I want to say well done.'

OK. I stretch out my hand to meet hers . . . it's so small! Elsa pulls me towards her and gives me a quick hug, stroking my head at the same time.

'Elsa, you're . . . small!'

I take a step back in surprise. Elsa is only a little taller than me. I hear her laugh. 'Why, how tall did you think I was?'

'I don't know, but from your voice I would've said at least one metre ninety!'

'One metre ninety, me? Oh, Mafalda, do you know what I think? That you can see my soul.'

'Soul? What do you mean?' I ask, stroking Ernesto's head. He's snoring already.

'That you see the contours of people's souls. That's different from the outline of their bodies. Sometimes they're bigger, sometimes they're smaller. I'm not surprised you see them. People with eyes like yours have magical powers.'

We sit close to each other, legs crossed. She takes the aspirin with a bottle of water. I hear the sound of the plastic. Surprised, I say, 'No one's ever said I have magic powers before.'

'Really? Well, now you know. There are lots of free-spirited peoples around the world who would see something very special in you Mafalda. People who would recognise that you can talk to the spirits of nature better than anyone else.'

'It's true, I talk to Ottimo. And to my tree.'

'Indeed.'

I sit in silence.

'You should go now. Your mum will be worried. Mafalda . . .'

'Yes?'

Elsa's voice turns suddenly soft and sweet. It sounds like it's floating to me on the wing of a seagull, weightless, sad, different from usual. As if it's coming from someone else, maybe the person hidden under all those floaty, incense-scented clothes. 'Mafalda, is my soul really that big? One metre ninety? Is that how you see it?'

I turn to look at her. I can't see anything of the physical Elsa. Just a lot of black.

I smile. 'Yes, it really is that big. I swear. Like a tree in full blossom. And, now that I look more closely, it's actually about two metres tall!'

'Thank you. I could never have hoped for as much. No one has ever told me I have a huge soul. Just once in my life, I wanted to know what that feels like.'

Click.

If they can't cure my eyes, I'll have to make up a new language, made of back-to-front words that make sense

*to everyone. A language for everyone and for weird people
like me, in other words.*

'Can you type Luigi's address into the maps please. I'm
just guessing at the moment.'

Mum is driving me to Luigi's – he's the editor of *Panino*
– because I still have to give him my commentary and
interviews from the race.

We get there in five minutes. The great thing about
our town is that it's not really a town, more of a village.
We all live fairly close.

This is also not so great. If you want some time alone
or to keep something to yourself, it's difficult, because
in a matter of minutes someone will be knocking at the
door asking if it's true what happened to you.

My aunt was once out in her garden with Ottimo
Turcaret. We were moving, which is why she was looking
after him. Well, she went outside and put sunglasses on
Ottimo. That might seem a bit weird, but she wanted
to protect him from UV rays because he'd just had cat
conjunctivitis.

One of the neighbours saw her and thought she'd
gone mad. My aunt told me that she'd been in the
queue at the supermarket a few days later and had
overheard two woman in front of her talking. 'Did
you hear about the woman whose cat goes surfing?'
they said. 'She forces it to, people are saying, and has
even made it a wetsuit.'

'No, poor creature. But how does it go surfing? Does it have a little cat-size board?'

'No, my son says she took the wheels off a skateboard and used that but, if you ask me, I think she puts the cat on a toilet lid. Last week I saw her at the recycling centre and that's what she was holding, a toilet lid!'

'What is the world coming to . . .'

Auntie told me she'd actually taken an old ironing board to the dump and it had never, ever crossed her mind to turn Ottimo into a surfer.

'We're here! I'll wait outside for you.' Mum interrupts my thoughts.

I ring Luigi to get him to open the door.

'Great stuff,' he says when he's heard my interviews with the runners. 'I'll transcribe them and put them in the next edition.'

'How did you get on?'

'I came thirtieth.'

'Well done. That's not too bad.'

'Oh, pull the other one! I'm useless at running.'

'Well, let's look at it from a different perspective. That's the same as coming third out of ten.'

'It doesn't sound so bad when you put it like that! Listen, have you any announcements for *Panino*? We've not got many this month.'

'What kind of announcement?'

'Anything really. Even a declaration of love would do.'

'Oh no, you can forget that!'

'OK, maybe a request for a book, someone to help with homework?'

'Hang on a sec. There is something . . . Can I put in an ad for my dad?'

'Of course. Is he out of work?'

'Yes.'

'Mine too. Right, what do you want it to say?'

'Giovanni, thirty-nine years of age . . .'

10

Aww, I Miss Colour

'Mum!'

That dream again. All the dancing girls in their floaty, colourful clothes, I'm up the tree, they go away, Ottimo goes away as well, only this time I slip on a branch. I let myself fall back and don't even scream.

As I fall, I see the stars.

I fan my face with the sheet. The dream brought me out in a sweat. It's getting warmer now, too. The cherry tree must be full of gorgeous blossom.

Aww, I miss colour.

'Mum.'

There's no point calling her. I remember she was going out with her friends tonight, the few she has left. Because of me and Dad, she doesn't have much time for them any more.

I've been calling out for her since I was little, even for the silliest of reasons. Day and night. She needs to sleep as well. It's just that, I know I'm thirteen now, but Mum will always be my mum.

I get up. A glass of water to calm me down then I'll go back to bed.

I take a jug out of the fridge. Our kitchen must be a nice blue colour at night, all lit up by the moon when we forget to pull the shutters down. Mum never forgets because she's scared of burglars. Only tonight, it's just Dad and I. Oh, what's that? I can smell fresh air, so not only are the shutters up, the window is open, too.

'Dad?'

A voice, on the balcony. Mine. What's going on?

I go outside. The scent of sea and sand swathes my face – Dad's tears. And it *is* my voice that I heard. My words are coming out of the recorder, floating down from the balcony like weeping flowers.

Click. The recorder is switched off.

Has Dad heard everything I said about him? That I'm tired of it all, that I asked Grandma – his mum who died years ago – for help? No, no, no! I didn't mean for him to know how worried I am.

'Dad, please, no . . .'

'Don't say anything, Mafalda. Come over here,' he says in a calm voice.

Two quick steps and I'm in his arms, and his tears fall on my head, just like two years ago when I ran away and he found me in the cherry tree.

This time it's Dad who has vanished; what I mean is, he's there in his darkened room but for me he's gone. Is he back now? I don't know. I honestly think it will take time before I really know. For now, I'm here in his arms. Whatever happens tomorrow, I'll deal with tomorrow.

'So you met the girl from your dreams?'

Dad and I are still awake, out on the balcony. It's 2 a.m. (gosh, Mum really is living it up tonight!). We brought out four chairs, two to sit on and two for our feet, and two massive – and I mean massive – bowls of ice cream.

We talked. We're still talking. It's as if a basket has burst in Dad, a basket that was full of coloured balls, and now I see them – imagine them – rolling out of the broken basket and bouncing around us.

I tell him everything that's happened to me these past few months. Everything except the job ad I put in our school magazine for him. I'm not sure yet if that was a wise decision.

'Yes. Her name is Elsa.'

Dad scrapes the sides of his ice-cream bowl with his spoon. 'Click, clack.' I haven't heard him eat like that in ages!

'That girl in your dream, do you know who I think she is?'

'Who?'

'You.'

I freeze, spoon mid-air. 'Me? That's impossible. She's older. And I'm not that brave or confident, plus I don't have such long hair. There's nothing about me that's like her.'

'You have such a huge soul, of that I'm sure. Don't ignore it. Listen to it! You'll regret it if you don't.'

'But what am I supposed to do, Dad? I'm only thirteen! I can't listen to souls. All I listen to is my voice in my recorder.'

'Well, record yourself, then! Make a list of all the things you can do without your eyes, right now, right here, and record it. This is it, Mafalda, the life you're living. The day in, day out, whether you're young or old, or in-between like you are now. You can't put life on hold until you're taller, until you're eighteen, or thirty. You can't wait to start making your dreams come true. Or even to have dreams. You need to do it now, use what you've got. You don't want to end up like me, do you?'

He smiles.

I cry this time, no sobbing though, just allowing the tears to run down my face, warm me, relax me. Yes, it's relaxing to cry into a bowl of ice cream.

'I made a list like that once.'

'Well, I think you need to find it.'

'Who's making all this ruckus in the garden at night?' Nino croaks from the upstairs balcony.

'Go back inside Mr Rossi, it's cold. Mafalda and I are going inside now so we won't disturb you any longer.'

Nino shuffles to the edge of his balcony. 'I was sleeping. And the cold in March will hardly kill me. I am wearing my dressing gown.'

'The dark red one, Nino?' I ask, head back, nose pointing up.

'The very one. What list were you people talking about?'

'My list of dreams.'

Nino clicks his tongue and drums on the railings with his fingers. In grandpa language, I think that means something akin to, 'do the boogie-woogie!'

'Well, maybe one day you'll let me see it, if I'm not dead already . . .'

'Nino, don't say that!'

'Oh, keep your hair on. Where's the problem? If these dreams of yours are big enough, they'll find me one day wherever I am, and I won't have any trouble recognising them as yours. I'll see them realised and say, that dream belonged to Mafalda! How far she's come, that girl. There's only one thing, though, that would upset me.'

'What's that, Grandpa Nino?'

'Not to be able to tell you how beautiful you've become,' says Nino, his words reaching me on a big soft cushion of kindness.

11

And the Winner Is . . .

'And the winner is . . .'

Silence in the classroom. There's a first time for everything. The teacher is reading out the winners of the reading competition. Me and Grandpa Nino compiled five book reports in total. Five novels out of ten in the teacher's list. That's not too bad, is it?

'Marco Valenti wins with a total of six books read! Well done!'

Applause. Marco Valenti? Who would've thought. Pity. I thought I might win. However, if he won with six books, that means I might be second!

'Mafalda, come and collect your certificate for second place.'

I did. More applause. I bet Debbie isn't even pretending to clap.

Who cares. As soon as the bell rings, I'll run home to

show Grandpa Nino my certificate!

'It's time. Let me through, I'm off home!'

Outside, fresh air, freedom!

I get home really quickly, pull the gate closed behind me, hear the voice of Emilia, the red-haired girl in year nine, saying hello as she walks past.

What's all that yelling? And the dog barking really loudly? And the siren . . . has someone been arrested? The commotion is coming from the road on the other side of our garden, behind the shed, parallel to the school.

I ask Emilia if she can see the police. She comes back to our gate but feels taller; I realise she must be up on the wall, holding on to the railings to get a better view. 'Not the police, it's an ambulance. Looks like they're taking someone away . . . oh, it's that weird hippy woman who sells bracelets by the church – know the one?'

'What? Elsa?' I run towards the commotion, even remembering to jump over the troublesome tree root at exactly the right time. 'Elsa!'

The police siren blares a few more times then stops; the dog keeps barking, the noise coming at me from all sides. Ernesto. I grip the railings on the back gate, I call out to him, implore him to calm down. 'Elsa, what's wrong?'

'Elsa, yes, that's me . . . is that my little girl?'

Her coffee-coloured voice now sounds more milky coffee. She's lost, agitated. It scares me. A man, a nurse maybe, asks if I know Elsa.

'Yes, of course.'

'Are you her daughter?'

'No, but . . .'

'Do you know where her daughter lives? She keeps talking about a girl, her little girl.'

I'm suddenly engulfed in sadness and don't know what to say. I shake my head, then I hear the ambulance doors bang shut and Elsa's voice disappears. The nurse climbs inside and turns on the engine.

'Wait! Where are you taking her?'

'We're going straight to accident and emergency.'

'And then?'

'She'll be found a place in a clinic somewhere.'

The ambulance drives away. I don't really know what a clinic is, but my heart aches thinking about Elsa alone on the stretcher, maybe with her wrists bound.

I let go the railings and lean back to get down from the wall.

Hey! What on . . .? Something licks my hand.

'Ernesto!'

I kneel down and throw my arms around his neck and nuzzle my face into the fur behind his ears. He whimpers softly.

'I'll find you a nice home until Elsa comes back, I promise!'

Then I think of Pip and his escaped convict, Magwitch, who'd run away from a forced labour camp, and I wonder if such a friendship, between child and prisoner, between me and Elsa, can exist in real life, or only in books.

Click.

Today, first of May, I, Mafalda, age thirteen and a half, am getting married.

I haven't spoken to Filippo since I went to see his English teacher and told her I think he's dyslexic.

Every now and then I hear what he's up to from his friends: yes, he's taking the tests and exercises that have been adapted for him, his marks are going up, he will most likely pass the year. But there's been no progress in the two of us either meeting up or making up. I've written him so many messages, recorded audio messages on WhatsApp but deleted all of them before sending them.

I don't know why. It would be so simple to just call him and say, 'Hey, shall we go and grab a pizza in our usual place?' But the truth is, it's not that simple. It's super-complicated. You can't bury something, move on, pretend like it didn't happen. Or he definitely can't, that much I know.

Oh, I miss him so much.

So Filippo, I get it, I'll make the first move. Even though it's the men who're always the brave ones in books and I could always just sit tight and wait. But no, I'll send you a message, to remind you what day it is today. It's Mafalda here, blind, messy and a smart cookie, or so I've been told, and no longer scared of being special.

Hiya. I wanted to say sorry for . . . everything that's happened, and if you're still with Debbie, I . . .

No. That's no good. Deleted.

Ottimo Turcaret comes over for a pet, rubbing up against my hands, which are still holding my mobile phone.

In the end, I write just five words.

You are essential to me.

Send.

Too soppy? Maybe. I feel stupid and a bit crazy, a child and also a young woman. I feel hot, my hands are cold. I wish I'd never sent the message but I hope he reads it.

Hugging my knees, I lean back and rest my head in the darkest darkness, silently screaming about something that feels awfully like fear yet, all things considered, is much, much nicer.

Midday. The church clock strikes the first of its sixty chimes.

I'm standing below the cherry tree, or below the branches that stretch outside the school grounds, casting their shadow over the street. I'm alone and I'm waiting for Filippo.

The sky clouds over and suddenly it starts to rain, soft at first but quickly heavier and heavier (the forecast said there'd be a storm today, but if you ask me, this is Elsa's handiwork – she's doing a rain dance in a meadow in Arizona somewhere. That's how I imagine her.)

The bell continues to chime – thirty dongs, thirty-one . . .

Then I hear him. He approaches slowly, walking quietly in the rain. But I can hear him. The splashing water drowns out his smell of trouble, but I know he's here.

Filippo.

My best friend.

He stops in front of me.

'You came.'

'Of course I came. What did you think?'

It really is him. Hands in pockets, glasses splattered with raindrops. That's how he'd look if only I could see him. 'You're wearing your hippy headband.'

'Yes. I have a gift for you, too.'

I dig into my jeans pocket and pull out the bracelet with the tree charm and show it to him. He accepts it without saying anything.

From the branches of the cherry tree, the watery fragrance of fresh blossom wafts over us. We're drenched by now but it doesn't matter. The rain is so heavy we can hardly hear each other speak, but it doesn't matter.

Me and Filippo are together again.

I don't know if we'll marry or just be best friends, maybe both.

I'm happy to be with him, here, now. Whatever happens tomorrow, we'll deal with that tomorrow.

As I think all this, I feel a kiss skim my face, landing somewhere between my cheek and mouth. Not perfect as first kisses go, but if you don't try, you'll never know, eh?

Evening. The window's open over the garden. It already smells of summer. I listen to the hum of the first cicadas. From the upstairs balcony I hear a familiar whimper. Ernesto has heard the cicadas, too.

'Good boy, there's a good boy.'

Grandpa Nino growls in his usual croaky voice, but it's just a pretence. It was love at first sight between him and Ernesto.

'I always wanted a dog,' he said, although he knows Ernesto's just on loan. He'll go back to Elsa as soon as she's well again. Hearing Grandpa Nino's voice so content made me really happy. It was like the voice of a child. All candy floss and hazelnuts.

The ringtone on my phone. Who can be calling at this time of day?

'Hello?'

'Hello. Uh, apologies for ringing so late. I'm looking for Giovanni.'

'I'm his daughter.'

'Was it you who put the ad in the school newspaper?'

'Yes, I did. Who am I speaking to?'

'My name's Giuliana – my daughter Daphne is in your year. Do you know her?'

'Not very well.'

'Yes, I don't think you've ever been in the same class. Listen, I'd like to speak to your father. I was really taken with the ad and my husband and I might have a job for him. Can you put him on?'

'Mafalda, phone!'

Mum's shouting at me from our kitchen balcony. She'll wake Nino and the dog!

I drop the big watering can beside the fig plant and run.

No one phones us on the landline any more, Dad was even thinking of getting rid of it. I like a phone with a receiver to pick up. I answer.

'Mafalda, it's Elsa. How are you?'

My heart lurches to my knees. 'Elsa, where are you?'

'I'm still in hospital. Not the one they brought me to originally, a month ago.'

'Where? I want to come and visit you!'

'Best not to. How are you?'

'I'm fine. I found a home for Ernesto. So don't worry, we'll look after him for you. When will you be coming back to get him?'

'I think it's going to take a while. I've got a bad case of pneumonia that needs treating. It's been a cold winter this year and if you hadn't let me sleep in your shed, it could have been much worse. I trust you, Mafalda. You're a smart cookie, I expect great things from you.'

As Elsa speaks, tiny tears begin to wet my cheeks, growing cold where they stop. She says other things and more tiny tears trickle out. I dry them on the back of my hand and wish I could tell her that I thought it would be different, that my life would be different at thirteen. Maybe I expected my eyes to be cured. I hoped, believed, they would.

'Elsa, I'm scared.'

'I'm scared, too. Listen, how about we write a list of our fears. Then we'll share it with each other. And if you're wondering how to find me, don't worry, I'll find you. I'll be back in town, sooner or later. But Mafalda . . .'

'Yes?'

'There's something else I expect from you, as well as the list of fears.'

'What?'

'Your list of dreams.'

Dreams

1. To be special.
2. To have friends (Filippo, Mum and Dad, Ottimo Turcaret, and other friends I've yet to make).
3. Go to America on a plane, run in a meadow.
4. Find an amazing job.
5. Finish my book.
6.
7.
8.
9.
10.

Click.

What did Elsa say? It takes at least ten dreams for one to come true. I have five already, which means I'm halfway there.

I'll have to think very, very carefully about the next five. I don't know if I'll know what they are by the end of the year. Maybe I won't even know before the end of high school or university, if I decide to go. It will be hard to recognise them in the dark, like finding the stars in a cloudy sky.

'Mafalda, Dad has hung up your dreamcatcher! Come and see!'

. . . if I don't find them, I'm sure they'll find me. It might take time but one day, my dreams and I will meet. I promise. As sure as my name is Mafalda.